Diamond Blood

Words by
Eric Danhoff

Artwork by
Cassandra Danhoff

What follows this are fairy tales and lullabies. These stories are my dreams and nightmares. These words are my ambitions and failures. These words are for my brother Danny, my family across oceans and here in arms reach.

And for Cassandra,
The brightest light I have ever known.

Diamond Blood

1. a graveyard of you

2. worm

3. scorched earth signature

4. weak

5. the maiden in the moon

6. we speak in video games

7. little bones

8. ertrinkender

9. the house of the black

10. a bird landed on my window

11. the emperor of sand

12. diamond blood

A Graveyard of You

The sensor is driving me crazy. I twist on the handle of the wrench until I feel a tear in the glove. My hands are not strong enough for this work. The hangar smells of hot oil. Bodies move in and out of the entryway to the commissary. The constant motion is too much. The sensor sings its tones enough to loop into a song. Ships dot the black space with brilliant colors. Mine was a simple red among many more dashed with paints and varied shades. I don't remember the name of this place. The path is dotted with the traffic of countless fleets. Easy to find. A place to regroup between the hunters, the traders and the pirates.

There is laughter from the left side. I can hear them going back and forth on the worth of my ship and tools. Another pull and shielding for the thruster is set. I can feel the steel cut the skin. My hand is bleeding. This will make it worse. There's so much noise in the bay. They have the faces of snakes. My blood has a scent. I can hear the rattle of their tongues as they plan the attack. I smack the wrench hard against the floor, enough to cut the siren song and scatter my tools. My eyes remain on the ship. they laugh again.

"Graysho kein bo kai ma wah?"

I don't know their language completely, only a few words. I'd heard it before on a salvage trip. Some traders and myself jumped to a salt planet for crystal mining way back. A mammoth fell dead from overeating. The body had roasted out on a rare shoreline. The sunset in that distance matched the purple glow of it's intestine. Its bowels had emptied out and covered half the beach. Our mouths curved. Stomachs turned and twisted. Big graysho, they said.

"Ka la mo sein pu ket, ne?"

The snakes take a step forward. Both seven feet high. Hoods of scales smother rivers of muscles. Black holes where the eyes should be. Each mouth houses four sets of teeth. Lips curl back to show the back rows. I won't be able to beat them both without getting cut up. Their breath is loud now. My eyes go to the hall towards Medical. I calculate the steps, the time to ask and receive the antidote for their poisons. The gun's in the ship. I'll have to do with the wrench and hope the suit can stop their fangs for me to get some hits off their skulls.

"Graysho jee neh ah?"

A new voice from behind me. I don't register. The teeth in their mouths are dripping now. Snakes mouths open up as if they could consume me whole. They just may. The voice gets louder. The language is easier for me than snake. A trader appears, phlegm colored rubber, masked up and suited for toxic. He places a hand on my shoulder.

"They bet how long it takes to kill you. They say you are easy to break. Ki ma."

Like glass, he said. The snakes laugh and back up. I bring the wrench down. Trader says something to them. I loosen the grip on the tool.

"Quagga don't eat humans. The teeth are a show of respect. They like you."

I don't believe him. The snakes spit words back and forth with the yellow man.

"Humans break but they go back together. How you do that? They want to know."

Their eyes are deeper than darkness. My suit is reflected back at me; the boots, the gloves, the insulated coating. A sky blue painted a new bloodied shade in their eyes. I haven't seen myself in a long time.

"We wrap and treat the wounds until they close. We set the bones right the same way, and break them again if we have to."

Trader repeats in a slithered tongue. The Quagga shout and speak with busy hands.

"They say you all crazy. When they hurt they just cut off and it comes back. Human love pain, huh?"

I step back from the trio and tend to my gear.

"We can't get enough of it. Ko so. Graysho."

A collection of laughter fills the space of the hangar. The Quagga point at me and speak sinister words; all teeth and lips, what could be smiles. A moment passes, and they are suddenly gone. Trader now faces me at the tail of my ship. The dock is empty, save for us. The siren song has stopped.

"Quagga need more men in population. Maybe you stick around. Go on hunts."

They were women?

"If they try to eat you just spit on them. They said humans shoot poisons."

He hands me a tool that I missed, knocked back behind the thruster.

"Maybe. How about the toxic?"

Trader waves his hands.

"Nothing new. Rains and winds burn through suit faster now. Getting worse. Planets going against me. They fighting back against us thieves."

"Is that what we are?" I ask him. I load the tools into the ship. Still no noise. No one in here with us. The gun is close. I will keep it in the holster if I come back here.

"Ga-lie kgi nagh mysghi?"

Trader asks if I know his language. I tell him I do. He's a Nagh; people from the sunbelt systems; a thousand planets laid like jewelry under blinding bright stars. Nagh were born in extreme light, their bodies were formed like paper. I loosen my clenched fists. My language is too hard, he says. The hangar's never been this quiet before.

"We are thieves. You are not. I seen you around. You don't kill. Don't steal."

"I have killed before," I say. He isn't convinced.

"Drift. That's what you do, right?"

I want to ask him how long he's been watching me.

"What you looking for?"

"I wish I knew," I said.

I don't have an easy answer.

"That's the problem with human. You think you smart, think you know. But don't seek."

A body steps through the sensor. The sensor screams and the hangar's alive again. I need fuel. I'm losing patience, growing hungry. Cutting the conversation could make it hard for me to come back. He did help me, after all.

"What should I be looking for?" It's all I can ask without disrespecting him.

"Come to sunbelt. We found something in the markets. It's got your language on it."

"You can't decipher it?" I ask.

"Not these words. Too big. Too weird. It needs a human. No one wants to buy it. So you can have it."

Sunbelt systems would be five days travel, at least. The ship will need cells to warp.

"Got cells? My ship isn't ready for that, at the moment," I say.

The Nagh takes me to his vessel in the corner. His storage pod is flooded with them. Just some of the spoils of constant trading. Maybe some taken by force.

"Take what you need," he says.

"Do we have to go now?" I ask. The Nagh shifts his shoulders.

"Up to you. Follow me if you want. More dangerous alone. My people don't know slow. We eat the babies if they don't move right away."

There's an awkward silence as I realize there wasn't a joke.

"Better get going," he says.

In minutes, we're gone from the hangar. A thousand lights and stones mark the way towards the sunbelt. I check the provisions again and again to make sure there is enough food without diverting. The Nagh can hold liquid in their throats for days before ingesting. He won't need to stop for anything. I took enough cells for six months of warp travel. He didn't seem to mind. There's at least five planets in this system that I want to check out. Before we hit the gate, I scribble the coordinates across my window. The Nagh has my attention. What is this object covered in my words?

The thrusters kick up and the stars and stones vanish. Light bends as the ship ignites with fresh uranium. The Nagh's ship is gone from my periphery. Warp is always dangerous. If he is lost, I know the way to sunbelt regardless. The engine noise whirls and spins into drones of singing machinery, then stops. The silence of space replaces everything. A quiet shaking rocks the ship and I into a lull. The need for sleep rests on my neck. It pushes me back to my seat. It takes my feet and places them on the dash. There is a pulse to moving thousands of miles in seconds. There's music. Brushes of wood hitting strings that shimmer and echo between the ears. They ebb and flow to the rhythms in my veins and the forceful blood beat of those drums. I can feel them in my bones. The sound is coursing through the body, pushing me forward. I wonder if the Nagh hears it too. I wonder if anyone does.

The first string of sunbelt planets dotted the bottom of this new sun with a beautiful symmetry. They are laid out with an architect's hand. There's fire everywhere. The system is illuminated with a silent explosion. The detonations carry out with strange precision across the surface of the star. It moves and reaches out with blades of flames only to dissipate and return to its source. A sole station sits between a storm of asteroids and a series of moons too small for more than a handful of ships to rest on. I feel the pull of the fire. Its invitation is strong. The Nagh's ship is suddenly in front of me. We both dock and look away from the sight of living fire holding court. Sunshields fall over the hangar, saving our eyes from the light.

"Follow," the Nagh says and heaves a giant pack onto his shoulders. He points to a trail of brown that curls around a corridor.

It leads me down stairwells caked in rust and shadow. An unknown light is coming from below, breaking through the dark and anxiety. Trash is kicked into corners, crafted into makeshift houses. I do not look to see if they are empty. Scales and discarded food fill the air with the smell of decay, this space is lived in. We are trespassing. The way goes down near the sounds of engines. I look to the Nagh and point back up. He waves his hand and points back down to the descent.

"Good stuff down here. You speak aO?"

I shake my head and check for my weapon. The aO were pirates.

"They don't know your language either," he says.

My grip loosens again. If the Nagh is leading me to a trap, he's done a great job of keeping me calm. The stairs cut right and we balance on old steel walkways. The grates reveal an army of gears and machines. This is the heart of the station. It spits bolts of energy that crackle and deafen.

The makers of the houses on the stairs reveal themselves and motion for us to follow. Steel doors open up by withered hands turning handcranks. New light pours in from a crack in the wall to cover us. Not just light now, but warmth. We enter. From the dark heart of the station, we step into a storage room glowing a soft gold.

"Undermarket," says the Nagh.

Tech and weapons are laid out on blankets. The makers hold their hands out, anticipating credits for their wares. The low lights reflect off chrome surfaces. The smell of smoke takes the oxygen from the room.

"How long have they kept this from the aO?" I ask.

"It moves from place to place. aO run this quad. Old Nagh that can't work, can't fight, take the scraps and hide. Good money for soldier's clothes and gear."

I thought of the trail that led me here. Behind me were hooded Nagh wiping it away with dirty rags. Their hands were small, nails torn away, palms and fingers bandaged heavy. I couldn't see their bodies underneath the clothing.

"Your people don't fight them? Take this back? The station is your home."

The Nagh shakes his head.

"I'm no soldier. Survivor. Better off in the toxic. Find and sell. Bring back here to them."

He opens his pack and brings them each a bag. Some open and ingest the contents. Others quickly cover their prizes and hide away. One of them motions for my gun. I show it to him. He lifts his hood slightly to review the weapon. Their skin was a burnt purple. White veins covered his neck like two hands holding his skin together. He licks the barrel and winces. When he turns to me, I see his face; eyes like teardrops, a slit for a mouth, two holes buried in the wrinkles that sucked air in. He runs for a bag and returns with a new rifle. I observe the new weapon. Good weight. Not too light on the handle. I turn on the sight. It works. The trader pulls me away from the merchant. He shouts for my gun.

"They're bringing it now," he says.

"Don't trade for that gun. He's been trying to get rid of it for months now. You give up your things too easily."

"Is your skin like that?" I ask.

He's quiet.

From the back of the room, old Nagh bring over a piece of a probe. They struggle with the weight. Sparks shoot out from the hole left behind. Reconnaissance equipment for scanning a large distance. It looks like severe cannon fire.

"The sun makes us. And it kills us. You don't know anything about that," he says.

The trader enters a few commands on the damaged keypad. The screen lights up. White numbers and symbols cascade across the cracked red sea, and then words. A stone lifts up from the hole left in the machine. He was right. They were mine.

"What punishments await the curious mind. Cell is born with no warnings. Yet it multiplies. Spreads across land. From a place unspoken, spills a desire. It comes not from a maker but a terrifying solitude. Cell is driven. There is a need. A purpose for the mark it leaves. Reason for the crushed things beneath its boot. A thousand words spoken. Repeated all hours. The words are in the air. The song is sung from the water. It hears the music the same as I. Will you seek."

"How did you find this?" I ask.

There is no reply.

I look at the trader. His suit is gone. A hood and long coat cover his burned body. He is damaged like all the others; white veins that creeped up around his head until they come together at his top like a crown.

"It came to the station itself. Programmed."

"And the stone?" I ask.

"We don't know what it made of."

"How can we not know what it is? The analyzers say nothing?"

"Thought it yours. We don't know much about your people. Last checkpoint was made from Nyzga. The center of sunbelt. Too hot for us. You take my suit. You go."

The suit was off his body. He's tired. The others clean then leave the suit at my feet, along with the rifle.

"Why not let the aO go first?" I ask.

"Don't know what's down there. Could be one of your people. We can't help. aO will hunt them down."

"How long has it been since you've seen another human like me?"

"Long time. But you don't want to go? How long's it been since you seen one of your own?"

I can't answer him. I don't know. I copy the coordinates, take the gear and head back towards the stairs. The golden light fades. No one walks beside me. I turn back to the Nagh. The trader is there somewhere. He's unrecognizable from the others now. I look for acknowledgement in their eyes. There is nothing. I raise a hand up. The heads turn away as the steel doors slam together. I'm alone in the darkness and lightning.

I ascend the stairs and leave the storming engine heart behind for my ship. The hangar is crowded with masks and hoods. A hundred faces look through me and disappear into the station. The bodies continue to enter and leave as if disappearing and reappearing in front of me. I'm lost to the noise and the flood. I keep the new gear hidden as I change into the Nagh's suit. No one questions it. No one notices me. I think about the words. For all the masks and suits and ships going the other direction, how many others were silent and searching?

The new weapon needs the right kind of ammunition. I head to the real market above the hangar and trade power cells for rifle rounds. The ship turns on with trepidation. The heat has ruined a bit of the igniter oil. I enter the coordinates for Nyzga. The shields open with loud bangs. The thousands inside the hangar take cover. White and red destroy the dark. I'm barreling towards a planet I've never been to.

Fire from the sun is too much. The helmet's vision protection still leaves a massive glowing ball that stretches over everything. I close my eyes. The words speak of music. I can hear the sounds. I cover myself from the gaze of the fire god. The trader shed his facade when I read the message. He didn't need to pretend. He wanted it gone. How long did it take him to find a human? What if I'm not the first one to try Nyzga? The engine's temperature pushed to red the closer the ship got to the planet. The strings of moons and asteroids are far behind me now. Passing vessels disappear from sight. There's only the fire and the planet that spins beneath the hands of flame.

Nyzga is the color of blood. I can see plant life, rivers, twisted and changed by fire. Warning lights tell me the ship is risking explosion. The air leaves my lungs. The part of me too afraid to move forward is still. I release the thruster and engage warp. I time it carefully. The engine skips and spits before throwing me into the planet's stratosphere. The blood planet moves towards the glass of the ship and pushes me back.

I vomit into my suit. The thruster is gone. The ship is floating. I guide it down towards a forest clearing. The hull crashes into a group of trees. Branches shaped by fire look like the arms of the Nagh. They pull the ship close and bring it to a stop. Sweat collects on my neck and chest. Thick clouds of orange protect me from the reach of the sun. The land is covered in mutated trees and grass. A river of white glides across a mountain of stone.

The rifle is ready. The ship tells me the source of the probe is a month's walk. I open the door and step out onto Nyzga. There are no signs of organic life. The ship needs to get back into the air. There's only enough food for a few more days. A fair wind blows through the grass. A few blades come loose and hit my visor. I watch as each one slowly disintegrates. The scanners say there are trace amounts of carbon and oxygen within the trees.

I walk to the river to collect some of the liquid. The suit is struggling to keep my temperature down. The rifle has a setting for mining. I test the beam on the river. The cut into the bank is strong. The water is thin and falls into the trench before flowing over and back onto its path. I collect some of the liquid and sever a piece of the closest tree and feed them into the converter in my pack. It draws out the elements and delivers them to me in a new form; fuel for the suit's temperature control. The engine oil is synthetic but a more primitive version can be crafted from the same sources.

I break to eat and rest. Time seems to be frozen here. There are distant moons in the Nyzga sky but often hide away behind distorted clouds. Hours pass, I believe. I don't sleep. The sun never moves so the light is always present, sometimes breaking through and casting everything in white. Within a day's time, the ship is able to move again. I follow the trail set. The river lines weave in and out of barren mountains and damaged treelines. Far off in the distance, I see creatures with wings to carry them. They're shrouded in the dust of the clouds. I hesitate to follow them before seeing how off the trail I would become. The creatures do not return.

The coordinates bring the ship to an abandoned settlement. Three houses set along a base of operations. Two vehicles sit idle around a single outline of arms and legs. I lower the ship to the settlement and approach. At the side of each house, equipment that shot up from the ground. Terraforming. They had to be settlers. The arms and legs in the center of the scene were attached to no face. A skull sits bleached and changed by the unending sun. The houses are empty; single beds, no personal items. Perhaps military. The base doors are locked off. The beam on the rifle cuts it after 4 tries.

"Emergency protocol activated."

The base A.I. repeats the phrase over and over. There's no sign of a struggle, only a trail that led me to a dozen bodies in the communications room. Women and children. Their uniforms were blue, patches and identifiers removed. Their faces were gone. There was no blood but someone removed the skin from their skulls. No marks from a blade either. The logs were standard reporting of changes to the nearby environment.

The names were unfamiliar. The way they talked was different too. Commanders remarked on their progress and wanted to know more. The crew consisted of several families. Initial logs are dated from last year but soon stopped. Commanding officers reach out for updates once the reports stop. There was extended inactivity besides the automated checks from terraforming machines. Rescue crews dotted their arrival but no exits. There was only one transmission since the drop off point.

"Drop a stone into a pond. The ripples echo out across the water. They do not stop even if you cease to see it. Cell walks across an entire planet and dies. Another is born to walk those same steps. The path is made for others to follow. What do you feel when you walk this graveyard of you? Do you know what a dead man is? He is the impression. Trapped to walk the same circle. Ripple across the same water. This is the song. The water sings of the dead, of those still living. The water sings of those yet to be born."

I can't feel my hands. Another stone appears with the words engraved. I run the analyzer. No results. No trace elements. It's a thin piece, a shard. A distress beacon suddenly activates. The sound shocks me from my trance. The ceiling of the base opens up to transmit. New coordinates are pointing to another planet deep in Quagga territory. It will take a week to get there. I don't have the tools to make the trip. I look back to the faceless families. There's too many to bury on my own. What is this feeling? It isn't fear.

Hours later, I'm back at the sunbelt station. Sunshields are up though the hangar is full. No one pays any mind to the flames. The blinding light still hurts me. The houses in the stairwells are gone. My footsteps echo louder than before. The way down to the engine room is empty. The heart of the station still beats. Bolts fire off like shots, filling the massive area with enough light to see traces of the machine.

The Undermarket is gone. The steel doors are sealed and closed off with spark fluid. There's nothing here but the relentless engines of the station. I stay in the Nagh suit. The smell of vomit has worsened since the red planet. I remove the helmet to empty my stomach and scoop out the remnants left inside the shell. I begin to wonder if I imagined the entire scene.

I'm clean but there is a faint smell. Nothing in my pack to mask it but converted water. I begin the ascent back to the hangar. The real market is scattered across a mile once past its heavily guarded checkpoint. Those watching over the market are Nagh soldiers. They're armored except for a patch across the head for the eyes to see out. They are not frail. The suits are tailored to outline their muscles, carefully built and trained. I remember what the trader told me about their bodies. Besides their weapons, the armor may be only for show. I consider hitting one of them to see if they would crumble. There's nothing here in the market but Nagh selling weapons and technology from the same tents I saw in the underbelly of the station.

There are entire families selling things. Children dance around me with guns and knives. No one says a word. Everyone is lost in chatter. The children pull at my hands and try to remove my gloves and boots. I walk in circles until I find another hunched over with bandaged hands. I grab them and whisper for the trader. They say nothing and vanish in a passing crowd.
Two more attempts. The same result. I lose my patience and head back for the ship. I am pushed into a tent. Three Nagh pull their hoods. One of them speaks;

"What do you want?"

"I found the source of the probe. Dead families. Someone took their faces," I say.

The Nagh do not react. I show them the stone and the shard. They move away from me.

"You shouldn't have come back."

"This is a trap I'm telling you. The probe led me to nothing and now it wants me to reply to another distress call?"

More Nagh enter the tent. I'm surrounded.

"Not just men but the women and children too. Did you take their faces?"

"You shouldn't have come back. aO may be coming for you," they say.

"Why would they be interested in this? I thought they didn't care about humans?"

"Follow us. Get on ship and go," they say.

I slam my fist into the wall and show them the coordinates.

"Tell me about this place. Where is this taking me?"

The Nagh are silent then begin to leave the tent and disappear. There is only one left. It reads the message and looks back at me.

"Plia. Quagga planet. No one live there. aO saw you leave. They're looking for you now. aO want the stone."

"How long have you had this thing?" I ask.

"Long time. You go now."

"Why are you so afraid of it? No one knows what it's worth. Why come after me?"

The Nagh slowly goes to leave the tent. I stop it with the point of my gun in its back.

"Am I the first one to come back from Nyzga?"

"Many others go. They don't come back. They watching to see what was there. Now they know. They see the beacon. We all see it. You really want to know what is out there? You have to be faster than them now."

I put the gun down.

"Is this a test?" I ask.

"You the only human we see in years. You know the words. We see it in your eyes. It talks to you. The words only for you. Don't know what it could be. Might be more just like you. Might be something good. Might be something bad. We don't want to know. We want it gone. Take it and go."

I look down for a moment and the Nagh is gone. I trade some cells for everything I need to make the trip to Plia. I make sure no one follows me out from the market back into the hangar. I set the course for the planet and sleep.

My darkness is interrupted by the words on the stone and shard. The voice in the dream is new. She sings the engravings. They fall and rise. The wood returns to hit those familiar strings. The sounds of pounding drums return to match my elevated heartbeat. The sounds of the water coalesce and become an ocean.

My eyes open to the planet. The ship's autopilot brought me safely to the nearest trading post. I step out and greet the Quagga merchants. The sky is dead. The sun has not yet risen. Muted blue cuts across the cascade of stars above us. A dark green aurora stabs the night. I show them the stones and the notes of the distress beacon. Their eyes open and their teeth reflect the starlight. The merchants point over the horizon. I can see a single moon in the distance just beyond the skyline. I hold my hand out to see if one of them will accompany me. They do nothing but stare through me. I re-enter the ship and barrel towards the unknown.

The ship jets over rolling hills and valleys. Flora and fauna are scaled and massive. Animals fly over fields casting intense shadows and calling out in foreign tongues. I can see them this time; scales like the Quagga but wings that look to be crafted from marble. Bleeding vines stretch across nearly every gap in the dirt colored rock. Behind me I can see a freighter orbiting the trading post. It has to be the aO. The traders were not lying. They were hunting me, the stones or whatever was pulling me forward. I eat the last of my food. The water in my pack is gone. The scanner paints a strange picture of Plia. A single body of water for an entire planet full of plants and healthy creatures. The marker brings the ship a few miles off the coast of this solitary sea. I land the ship and exit. The sound of the freighter echoes in the distance. I reload the rifle and my sidearm.

The miles disappear quickly with baited breath and steps crunching blue leaves. The lay of the land moves with strange precision. Flat ground disappears to giant holes leading down into some untold emptiness. I see nothing when I look down. Every moment I stop is followed by a nervous glance back towards where I came. I am waiting for steps other than mine. I hear no voices, no gunfire. There is no wind here.

The sea is in my sight. A plateau of rock formations rise and curve around the coast. My pack is becoming heavy and I consider losing it somewhere recognizable to recover. A shot from an assault rifle cracks the peace of the valley. I am getting higher up, I notice. Another round grazes the rocks close by. They can see me. I move to the side and try to find another way to the water. The only way is up and over the rocks. The freighter materializes above my head. The aO is right on top of me.

The hunters emerge from the fields. Their uniforms shift in color to match their surroundings. They wear masks with air exchangers. I ditch the pack, pocket my wrench and the converter, and move serpentine along the base of the valley. Another massive hole stops me. I catch the edge of the cliff and pull myself up from falling in completely. I look down to see that underneath the surface was not a hard landing or spikes or other death but water.

A group of hunters approach. I find a set of rocks to hide behind. The aO are around my size, not too much bigger. A fight could be in my favor if I catch them by surprise. There are four of them. I set down the converter and it begins to take the carbon closest to it and change it into liquid. The hunters hear the noise. By the time they reach it, I am gone. The converter finishes its process, opens its chamber wide enough for the oil to ignite with the air. The burn comes quick, as do their screams. I learned a long time ago how to manufacture grenades using some earth, oil and ship fuel. I wait for their voices to fade. The freighter looms large over everything.

The water at the bottom of the well was black. I ready myself to jump. A shot from a custom automatic hits my arm. I return fire and it falls to the ground. The aO soldier curses in unknown language and crawls away from me. I don't have anything for my wound. The pain begins to travel to my head. I stumble but follow him instead. The aO does not speak. It coughs and spits a bright colored blood. It reaches for more guns. I quickly knock them away. The yellow fluid is pouring out of his stomach now. He does not have the strength to fight. My suit is stained red. I watch it fall to my hand. I wipe it before it hits the ground and marks my presence.

I stand over the soldier. It turns back around to face the night sky. Its breathing slows. I show my hands and pull the mask off. I don't want it to suffer any longer. It grabs at my hands but stops resisting. The air exchanger was connected to a tube. I pull three feet of tubing from the mask. The sky is darker now. I pull the mask off.

Behind it, was an unfinished face. A white mass of eyes and mouth and lines of skin disconnected from its neck. I sit there and hold its hand until all the air leaves him. I wait for him to expire. My fingers move for the spaces between its face. My hands pass through that open air as if his head was five scattered pieces, held together by some invisible thread. I check his wound to see there is no hole. The blood had come from some phantom spout, seemingly closed off now. This doesn't feel right. A sound of distant rumbling turns me back to the abyss behind my former enemy and I. The water is rising up and splashing onto the field. I approach carefully and peer over the edge. Black liquid has flooded the chasm and my reflection stares back at me, illuminated by distorted stars and the bent mirrors of auroras gliding across the sky.

The fields are so still. The wind has stopped. I wait for more sounds, more hunters with weapons firing and shouting for vengeance. There is nothing. I go to the bodies burned by my cloud of grenade fire. The bodies have changed shape. The arms and legs are jagged, pulled by some unseen force. Each of them have been cut apart, in clean but random angles. My hand closes through those spaces as well. Something is happening in this place. Something fantastic. Frightening.

The first soldier should not be left behind. I go back to him and carry his body to the newly formed pool of black. I lower him into the liquid. Something happens. His shape disappears. He does not submerge. He is taken and gone completely. I look closely. The water is a pitch black. The soldier has vanished. The level of the liquid rises. I question if loss of blood is pushing me into delirium. I bring the dead team to the same pool. One by one, I drop them in. Slowly, the water reaches its edge and flows over onto the field.

Is this the water of the words etched on those stones? The ones that speak to me in my sleep, in every step I have taken? I look to the pool again to find nothing. Deeper down, the water recedes. It drains silently down into a void. Then there is thunder. Not from the sky, but under my feet. A crack in the bedrock opens up. Fissures unveil and stretch out like limbs across the field and valley. The openings circle back and connect, forming angles and shapes until finally, a figure. Obscure. The pool beneath me moans unintelligible. A growl. A gleam from the bottom of the well. Moisture. A color. An eye.

I make for the pack across the field as the ground breaks behind me. The figure slowly shakes off crusted dirt and rock stuck to its body. Its numerous limbs extend out into the air, throwing stones across open land. The creature is gigantic. It hovers above the planet like a moon free of gravity. Its eyes blink tears of black water that crash down into the trenches made by its rise from the grave. The eyes slowly roll forward. A grouping of massive mouths open. Its endless teeth devour the freighter. No sound but the smashing of steel. Is this what I have been looking for? Is this what calls me? The creature does not see me. It's meal is finished. I watch it move towards the horizon. I retrieve the pack, turning back often to watch the creature stalk aimlessly. The planet is ripped open. Layers of rock and mineral bore down deep into new caves.All around me, the tears of the creature have made new puddles. I kick a broken rock across one of them. And I watch it fall under the black and disappear. The puddles still reflect me and the planet's painted furious sky. I make the choice and step into the water.

The world I stood on shifted. There is no darkness. My footing was gone for a split second, then returned. I find myself on the other side of the mirror. I look up to see the new sky of this second world, this hidden world. Twisted ripples flow out and disappear beyond my vision. The fields are a darkened neon, the cracks and fissures of the angry giant are replaced with fresh land. Everything is left of center somehow. The valley is here, the planet's hills and vines, all represented in this new realm, yet a few shades darker.

I walk forever. I wait for creatures, hunters, snakes, or dead men to descend upon me. A ship is there waiting, just like mine, colored blue and ready for takeoff. No caverns of eyes. There are no pools or black water. At the top of the valley was no coastline or sea. I am submerged. I'm beyond the planet. I'm inside the planet.

The grave of the alien is gone. In its place, a series of stones that lift high off the ground and curve. These stone veins form a new ghastly structure. The entryway is shrouded in unnerving empty space. My hands shake, trying to keep the rifle steady. From the negative space, there is a single flame lighting a thin walkway. I step carefully and inch towards the end of the path. I turn back to the beginning to see the mirror planet is gone. There's only me, the flame and the stones I walk on. The closer I am to the flame, my vision settles. The stone structure has changed again. Patterns and engravings are revealed as the fire intensifies. The walls tell stories to me. They speak of figures crossing miles upon miles to find millions dead. The bodies are stacked into stairs. They climb the dead and find themselves crowned kings and queens of an empire lost. The light burns clear and I follow.

I reach the end. There is a door. The fire is pulsing. Seductive. I feel an urge to wrap my hands around it. I choose to wrap on the door instead. It opens. Inside is a small chamber. A figure stands shrouded in strange colors. I cannot describe them.

Their shape morphs and pulses like the fire of the hall. Their hands are familiar. I have seen their bandages before. The hands pull back the hood. I study the veins and beady eyes of the alien.

"You're the one who brought me here," I say.

The Nagh says nothing in return.

"What are you?" My question is unanswered.

"This is only the beginning of the journey," it says.

"What is this place?" I ask.

Behind them, an unseen flame lights the chamber, revealing a map of galaxies, systems and planets. It fills the open air with tiny lights and spheres, all spinning and shining against the pulse of the flames.

"The walls are an illusion," it says.

"Press against the facade and watch it distort. It doesn't break. Opening is all you need."

"I don't know what that means. What facade?"

"Place your hand upon me and see yourself."

My blood runs cold. There is a strange energy in this room. The planets and stars pass through us both. I step towards him. His face is dead. I reach out to touch him. My fingers glance against his skin and he ripples. From a space behind his eyes, I pull another stone from him.

Like water, the ripple echoes out from his face into the dark. It twists the flames, the planets, the frame of the room and out into the hall. I fall to the floor.

What is this? Is this an illusion? A sculpture of water? I crawl back to the hall. The ripple carries on, stretching the stories etched on the stone like a wave.

"He's waiting for you," it says.

I can barely breathe.

"Who is he?!"

I don't turn back to him. The hall continues to pulse and settle. I get to my feet and head back to the beginning. I punch my chest to see if I ripple as well. My body is not a part of the water. I am simply swimming within it. How is this happening?

The questions chase me as fast as I run. The mirrored ship opens the same as my real one. I step inside and close the shield. A chill runs through my body. I see the moon, mirrored as everything else from the real planet. It stares back at me. I look to the third stone. It speaks.

"The water sings of you. Cell drifting in dead space. You can hear the song, even as it comes from your own mouth. The call for truth. To lift the veil. See what lies. Beyond the wall. Do you feel it? The drums that pound with the rhythm of your heart. The spires that strike against wires pulled tight. This is your song. This is body and blood. The wall is all but unbreakable. Facade stares back from the mirror. The illusion is you."

The engine fires and the ship controls the same as mine. I leave the mirror planet and set a course straight for the mirror moon. The flight is smooth. The ship has more fuel than I remember. The moon draws near. Something does not seem right. It looks flat. The ship grows closer and it feels like I'm colliding with a wall. There are no shadows. The empty space around it feels hand-drawn, painted on a surface.

I pull the ship back from hitting the moon. The darkness is littered with a thousand lights like stars. But they're not real. I can feel it. I put the ship into idle and I activate the emergency life support. The glass shield opens. My hand reaches out to touch the blackness. It stops at something. An invisible wall keeping me from falling out into the empty space. The stars, the moon, it is a facade. My fist crashes against this wall.

"Press against facade. Watch it distort."

I reach for the ship's controls. I edge it forward. The hull stops at the wall. The metal bends. My hand reaches for the moon and it stops at nothing. I run my fingers across an invisible wall. There are no gaps or holes. I'm trapped between a mirror and its edge. The black water feels like years from now. My foot never leaves the gas. The ship limps forward until the hull begins to bow. My hand pushes against the wall. I feel it give. I wait to be taken but there is no pull. My fingers disappear behind the painting and I pull it back.

Hunger pangs come from nowhere. I feel the sweat on the back of my neck. How long have I been in this mirror wandering? I reach for the stones. I grip them tight. The words are still there. The voice speaks louder than ever. What am I waiting for? What is there to run back to? I push my foot down on the accelerator. The ship struggles against the solid black. I press my fist against the wall again. I watch my arm disappear. My body follows.

The ship is locked between the mirror and the moon. It shatters and collapses on itself. The world around me moves away. I'm floating on the edge of nothing, standing on static. Grey half shapes stab out. Drawings of land and trees start, then fall away. My feet are steady, standing on empty air. Behind the wall, sat an incomplete space. I have fallen through so many worlds, I don't know how to begin turning back. There is no leaving this for the safety of quiet autopilot sleep, bargaining with traders or the ignorance of not knowing what lies behind the placeholder of what I knew as life.

The environment begins and ends, I can almost feel the hands of frustrated artists starting, then stopping. Along the trees, the beginnings of a house. My body pushes, moves without permission. The mind is unwilling, weary. I watch my body climb steps of air as solid as steel and sound the same. The house has no front door. Yet my hand still goes for a knob, grabs tight onto an object and turns. This door of nothing opens. I'm greeted by a suit, its gun metal color a stark contrast with the half of a house it stays in, tailored for harsh conditions. The room is an unfinished sketch.

A window with shaded sunlight. A broken television. A fireplace carrying carbon embers. And the suit. There is a body inside it. The arms move. The legs cross as if this person had been waiting for someone to step through.

"Was it anything like you imagined it would be?"

The voice came out as a deep murmur.

"I thought it would be treasure. Maybe a trap, an empty chest that clamps down on your hand."

"You're closer than you think," he said.

"Can you tell me what this place is?" I ask.

My voice broke into a whimper. I could not hide my fear any longer.

"What punishments await the curious mind? This is what brought you to me; the desire to know the truth of what we are," he said.

"And you know this truth?" I ask.

"I do. If you put the stones together, they make a key. Funny, isn't it? How things can seem so random, so strange but there is something that links it all together. There is design in everything we see. There is design in everything done by us, or to us."

"How many others have come this far?" I ask.

"You. There is only you."

"There's no going back, is there?"

"You won't have to go back," he says.

"What do you mean?"

"Do you know what a dead man is? He isn't just stuck in the impression he left behind. A ghost is the impression. A small moment of energy on infinite repeat."

"Are you saying we're dead?"

"Have you forgotten the bodies? The fear in the eyes of your alien journeymen? The distortions, the worlds hidden in mirrors, behind walls, the broken faces? We are all dead. We process death as a constant."

"All your doing?"

"You've been searching for a poet, a god that speaks to every doubt in your bones. The truth is none of those. The facade carries beyond the impossible ground you stand upon. No weapon of mine would dare take the life and face of a woman and child. I'm telling you now that you could pull the skin from your own face and still speak. You would feel nothing."

"I bleed. I feel pain," I mutter.

"You feel what you are programmed to feel. We have makers. I have seen them work for countless hours, only to wipe away entire civilizations with a careless arm. Our creation and destruction happens within seconds. The cycle is eternal. I have seen it. This house is my only escape from the erasure."

"And you left those stones to try and find someone else to escape? To keep you company?"

"To show them the truth of this place. To show them the hands operating the puppets...You feel it. You could never run from it."

"I don't want to run," I say.

I don't know if this is true.

"I've seen so many dead men line the ground and flood the fields with blood. I have seen a battlefield reset in a storm of white. A million killed and reborn to die again."

"The same music in your dreams I have heard for a lifetime. The blood beat of the drums, the strings that rise and fall when you travel. Where do you think it comes from? What if I told you everyone hears it. Do you still doubt me? Even after stepping through the mirror?"

I have had enough of the games.

"Take off your mask," I say.

There is a heavy laughter behind the suit.

"I'm not wearing one," he replies.

I can't help but step back.

"Are you sure?" I ask.

The body inside shifts. They move in directions aimless. He does not answer me. Had the thought ever crossed his mind? I go first. I hold my breath at first. My vision is clear. I exhale and suck in whatever is there. The air is breathable. I drop the helmet to the invisible ground and wait for the poet to follow.

His hands reach for the helmet. He lifts it high over his head. His face is mine.

"This is new," the man says. My face smiles back at me.

"What happens now?" I ask.

"The episode is about to end," it says.

Bullets cut through the house. A sudden invasion of aO appear in the negative space. I return fire and cover the poet. He laughs.

A grenade rolls to my feet. The blast throws us far away from the house. I cannot see him. Soldiers storm the nothing. Vision is failing. I don't feel my limbs. My hands and legs fall into the white. I cannot pull myself free. White lines cut through my suit and my body splits into new directions. Something rips me apart. Everything shakes. The mind says to crawl. The arms move in jagged unison.

The poet is still. Explosions echo across the blank space. I can hear the bullets. There is no fire. I want to call out to him but I don't know his name.

I can't remember my name.

Soldiers stop and turn in formation. I wait for them to finish us off. They move in place. Their eyes are dead. I have to keep going. I need to get out of here.

Don't fall asleep.

Don't let go.

Don't reset th-----

"That is crazy," said Nick.

The writer's room was frenzied.

"Yeah, the alien eating the ship is a good one," said Jeff.

"But I think we need to flesh out the exploration," said another.

Programmers took notes. Pads of paper were stacked on the table.

"Enemies drop in and firebomb the whole area," said one.

Black ink scrawled out multiple scenarios.

"But we need to finish the area to test the physics," said another.

The screens around them repeated the tests in a digital format. Bombs drops, bodies are thrown.

"The models still ragdoll like crazy when they blow up."

"The testers aren't giving us anything else. Just keep tweaking it until they don't break apart. The demo has got to be ready to go online by the end of the week."

The decision was made. A click of a mouse erased everything. No explosions, no bodies, no aliens or death. Fingers run across the keyboard. A final button is pressed. The hangar is drawn, square by square. First, the ships drop in perfect place throughout the floor. The pilots decorate the empty space. A man awakens with a tool in his hand. He remembers nothing. There is an annoying sound and there is work to be done.

"The sensor is driving me crazy. I twist on the handle of the wrench until I can feel a tear in the glove. My hands are not strong enough for this work."

Worm

"I had this dream where you were choking me."

The car was going too fast but the music was just the right volume to keep from edging Jay to slow down.

"In a weird way, I felt like I deserved it."

The dream he had described lingered in the dark spaces of the road and the clicks between the tracks of the cassette.

"So, I let you keep going. I stopped breathing, but I didn't die. I just kept watching you look right through me until I sank into the ground."

"Si," Jay cut him off.

"Sweet elixir, please."

The beer in the back was cold to the touch. Simon kept his own close to his leg in case cops pulled up. They'd been driving for an hour but they didn't have any other sounds. Jay flipped the tape to play side one over again. The guitar ripped on that second track. He brought the tape to his house days ago. They had yet to reach side two. Simon grabbed the case to study the cover; a man diving into a swimming pool surrounded by a dozen faces painted in black and white.

Jay didn't say a word. His head moved in sync with the drums.

The elixir began to take effect. That invisible grip on his neck seemed to loosen. He wanted to tell him more about the dream.

The third track started up.

Simon nodded and downed the rest of the can. He snuck it out the window and went for another. The party was invite only. They were taking a risk showing up being sophomores but they hoped the cans in the back would be enough. The house was in the rich part of town, according to the whispers of the girls in algebra class. This meant two very important things; a pool in the back and guest rooms.

The address and directions were quickly scribbled that morning on the back of Simon's notebook, half destroyed as it was, but they had found the house. It had three floors, a balcony, large glass windows that let you see everything inside. The lights from the pool had covered everything in neon blue, even the girls. Jay parked around the block of the cul de sac. He turned the car off, pulled the case of beer out and slung it over his shoulder. After two steps, he turned to Simon.

"Bring the tape. We may need it," he said.

Simon yanked the cassette and dropped it in his pocket. He looked at himself and his partner, both tragically underdressed for this social outing; Torn jeans, patched leather and their shirts doused with sweat. It was too late to go back now. They made their way to the gate in the back. The figures of blue moved in slow motion as they got closer. The girls were sculpted by the hands of an artist, each with small mountains of perfect symmetry. Every blue body that caught their eye was surrounded by groups in track jackets.

Jay rang the doorbell at the gate. Every head slowly turned to them. Simon waited for the laughter. It was a familiar feeling he had prepared for. Some smirks, but no dismissal. A girl stepped from the poolside to the gate. She covered herself with a towel. Her head cocked forward as if to ask what they wanted.

"We bring you the drink of the gods." Simon said as he held the case over his head like newfound treasure.

She said nothing. She looked down, turned and went back to the pool. The gate was left open. Victory.

The boys looked at each other, stepped through and disappeared into the mass of bodies. They navigated well enough with words to stay in their company. Simon tried not to look at Jay. The words from the dream had followed him there, even with beautiful eyes and legs dripping wet. He could feel his hands tightening, as if they were searching for something to grip.

Once the wind began to pick up, the girls brought them inside. The tape found its way to the rack system. The sounds of side one filled the rooms of the house. Conversations drifted as the faces revolved with the hands of the clock. Jay bounced through the halls. Simon stayed in the center and observed the chaos. He listened to the words and mostly said nothing in return. It was better this way, for him. The drink of the gods worked wonders for the atmosphere. The music stopped for a brief moment and new guitar lines cracked the murmurs of the party. Simon's ears perked up. This was side two.

The first song smashed through the faded voices. Someone new approached him. His heart had stopped.

"Who are you?" she asked.

"I don't know," said Simon.

"Should probably find out sometime."

Her hair was immaculate; black braids with parted bangs.

"I'll try my best."

She looked at him for a moment.

"You don't belong here," she said.

"None of us do."

Sylvia was her name. He had already known.

"Wonder who brought the music. The hostess seems more Sheena Easton than Def Leppard, doesn't she?"

"I did," he said.

"Good taste."

Her eyes kept him still. The nervous energy disappeared, replaced with a calm.

"Not into small talk?" she asked.

"Long moments of eye contact are better."

"Are you learning me?"

"I might be," he said.

She crossed his path in school before, always in tight leather and a Zeppelin shirt.

"Why are you here?" she asked.

"Lonely," he couldn't stop the word.

"Right place, then. Plenty of people trying to fill the void."

"Like you?" he asked.

Sylvia disappeared into the other room. Simon did not move. He wouldn't follow. The music was too good here. The beer seeped into his veins. The girl moved through the room again and again. Each time, she said nothing. The eyes had said so much with each passing glance. A random hand passed him something green, tightly rolled. He inhaled the smoke and closed his eyes for what felt like hours. Distorted guitar cut his peace and ripped his eyes open.

"Lady Strange," he mumbled to himself.

The people in the room had changed. Jay had materialized next to him. He was wired and talking too loud but Simon still smiled for him. He shouted into his ears about a girl he met on the patio and somehow, Sylvia stepped through the room as if by magic. She stopped at the stairs and turned to them. It was long enough for them both to realize who she had chosen. Simon did not look back at his friend. Jay sat back and rolled his eyes.

"All yours, man," he said.

Slowly, he got to his feet and climbed the stairs. Sylvia stretched her hand out and led him to a room. She shut the door behind them both. They fell into each other. He could see the outline of her face even without light. Both laughed as he picked away at her clothes. She was kind to his inexperience.

Even in her arms, the dream was there.

The thought of dying was a distant ache he could not forget. Good times with Jay did nothing to silence it. The liquids in his veins, the doses of chemicals to slow his blood, all were losing their strength. He remembered the weapon at home, the one with his father's name. It still called to him. The hallways of his home were as empty as the new schools every other year, as empty as his parents eyes.

But this, he thought, was different.

The void was gone.

Morning came too quickly. Simon stayed in her embrace, delaying the trip to the bathroom until she woke up. He told her the story of him and Jay as kids in the forest by the highway. They used to wait for heavy rain and run out to their spot with all these downed trees that never got replanted. They used to take off their shoes and walk in the mud, stepping over all the worms that pushed themselves through the soil.

They didn't speak much as they dressed. The floors downstairs were stained with mysterious liquid. The guest bedrooms could not contain the bodies strewn about the place. Sylvia held his hand as they snuck out the back door. Jay had slept in the car. Simon offered to drive her home. She kissed him sweetly and refused it.

"I got a ride," was all she said.

Sylvia slowly put on her shoes and began to walk down the street. The sounds of the highway washed over her footsteps.

"Don't wander too far from me."

"I won't," said Simon.

Jay didn't realize he'd forgotten the tape back at the house until they were already back home. Simon offered to go back but it was too late. The air that Sunday afternoon was too hot. Both looked at each other and figured nothing was waiting for them behind those doors. The boys stayed out. They got lost in the forest again like when they were little and found that patch of downed trees. This place belonged to them. It was a sanctuary from the bad days. They laid atop the broken branches like they did when they were younger and waited for the storm to come. After a few hours, clouds began to collide and the sounds of rain hitting the trees filled their ears. Simon thought of Sylvia. He couldn't wait to see her the next day. Jay asked him as much as he could stand to hear.

"There isn't much to tell. She was amazing," said Simon.

"That's good, man."

Both stayed in the storm until they were soaking wet. That night, Simon spoke nothing to the people at the dinner table. He did not think of the dream, nor the void. He did not think of the weapon. It was only her and the shadow that she cast.

Simon did not see Sylvia the following day.

After a few days, he started to ask around about her. The rumor was that she dropped out. Teachers said nothing about Sylvia. Calls to her home went unanswered. The school office never confirmed or denied that she dropped out. After a few weeks of not attending, she was expelled.

Was she in danger?

Did he get her in trouble?

Jay told him over and over that she had to be fine. He offered endless reasons for her leaving. Simon accepted none of them. There had to be a reason why she left. The rumors morphed and changed as the months went on. Some said that Sylvia was living in her own place around town, that she started work at a dollar store. Girls said that she had gotten fat and when they tried to go back to see her again, she would be gone. There were no addresses or phone numbers for her. No close relatives.

"Maybe she doesn't want to be found," Jay said one day. Simon never had an answer for those words.

A year had passed, then another.

The conversations always went the same.

"Why stay then?"

"People said she got fat. Maybe she got knocked up or something?"

"What if I am the father?" asked Simon.

"Dude, no. You're not the father."

"You don't know that. She could be out there right now, needing my help."

"We don't even know if she had a baby or not. This is all the words of cheerleaders. You can't trust cheerleaders."

The void soon returned. Nothing stopped the pain of not knowing what happened to her. Nothing felt the same.

Senior year was a slow hell. There was a constant need for people to know what he was going to do with his life, what was his next step. He could only think of Sylvia. When class ended, he would drive to the highway that took him to the party and walk the same steps as she did when wandering off. He wished he had thrown her into the car and taken her home. Jay bought another copy of the tape. Simon found it in his bag with a note;

"The only way to look back is when you're moving forward."

High school ended with fanfare and questions. He was a bystander in the lives of everyone around him; a hundred different television shows with the same plot twists. Others got jobs, enrolled in college courses, packed up and moved to other states. Simon was frozen in place. The voices at the dinner table got louder, more aggressive. He didn't have the answers they wanted. There wasn't a plan. He didn't know what his next step would be. Their faces were blank when they weren't shouting at him, or each other. He'd been watching them repeat the same pattern of painting a fake smile in mornings and returning at night, drained and empty. He would not become them. The dream of sinking into the ground with the worms returned. It gained details; the forest expanded way past his line of sight. Jay's hands felt stronger. He could feel the water staining his bare feet. When he sank into the dirt, the worms found their way into his mouth.
Simon would fall from his bed every night, coughing. He decided to find her.

Under the guise of looking for work, he hit the streets, checking every store he could reach with his bike. Jay had the car, and he was working at night. They hadn't spoken in a few weeks. Simon didn't blame him for wanting to move on. Sylvia was all he could return to. He couldn't forget her. Not until he knew she was okay. It was on the third day when he saw her.

She wore the uniform of a store clerk. Her hair was unwashed and tied back. No belly. He quickly stepped to her and spoke.

"Hi," she said.

Her voice was lower.

"Do you remember me?" he asked.

"Of course, I do."

She pulled a box cutter from her smock and began to tear into boxes of hair spray.

Simon waited for something more.

"You never came back to school."

"I know," she said.

"Where did you go? I didn't know where you lived and by the time I found out, the house was empty."

"I had a baby. Parents left right after," she said.

It was true. Simon's heart sank.

"I'm sorry."

"You did nothing wrong," she said. Sylvia said everything looking at the dust on the shelves. Simon stepped in front of her next row of boxes.

"Can you look at me? Like actually, look into my eyes?" he asked.

Sylvia blinked. Her movements seemed so different, stilted. She didn't refuse to move. It was like she didn't know how. Simon reached for her chin and pulled her face close to his.

"Better?" she asked.

The question felt so hollow. He searched her eyes for the same flame. It was there, buried. The eyes were different. They were darker.

He kissed her lips. Sylvia's face did not recoil. She accepted the kiss and nodded. He wanted to scream, to shake her, anything to pull more words from her mouth.

"When do you get off work?" he asked, shaking.

"Tonight at 8."

"Can I take you home?"

"You came here on a bike," she muttered.

"I want to come back tomorrow. Will you be here?"

Sylvia nodded.

Simon looked and saw her manager staring at them from the corner of the aisle. The top of the old man's head slowly tucked away behind the yellowed shelves.

"Do you still like me?"

"Yeah. But it's different now. I don't think you'll want to stay," she sighed.

"Try me."

Simon left the store, memorized the address. He rode home with new vigor, new energy in his steps. He told no one that he had found her. The moment belonged to him and he wanted no one's opinions to tear it down. She had a baby, but it didn't matter whether it was his or not. His heart pounded through the night until the following morning. The store manager looked him up and down as he moved through the aisles, laced with sweat. Sylvia waved her hand to let the old man know it was alright. She told him to come back at five, for lunch break. He waited and sweated through his clothes. She did not mind. He didn't have money but she had enough in her pockets for sodas at the ice cream stand down the street.

"You need money," she said.

He promised to get a job the next day.

"Why didn't you tell me about the baby?" he pressed.

"It happened really fast. I didn't tell anybody until he was born."

It was a boy. His heart stopped.

"Where do you live?"

"Close to the store. I walk," she said.

The sun began to go down when they took seats at a table outside the stand. There were kids all over the street, playing and screaming.

"Who's watching the baby?" he asked.

"No one," she said.

His head turned. The lampposts turned on and the city lights cut holes in the dark that slowly crept over them.

"What do you mean?"

"Nobody watches him. He doesn't need it," she said plainly.

"How is that possible? How old is he?"

"Two."

She didn't answer the other question. He did the math. It wasn't his kid.

"Who's the dad?"

Sylvia didn't answer. She looked out at the highway. It wasn't too far from where they parted the night of the party. Simon kissed her again. Sylvia only nodded.

"Do you still want to be with me?" he asked.

"I told you. It's different than before."

Sylvia turned away from him. She looked back towards the ground.

"The baby came to me from the forest."

Simon felt a chill go up his spine.

"The forest?"

"That's where he is now. I go to work, feed him and go home."

The kids on the street were suddenly gone. It was darker now. He looked all around him to make sure they were alone.

"Does he have a name?"

"Simon," she said as she smiled.

The soda fell from his hand and spilled out onto the concrete. This didn't feel real.

"Can I see him?" he asked.

"Tomorrow," she said.

She gripped his hand tight and walked away. Simon looked back at the night sky and turned. Sylvia had vanished. He rode home faster than before. What was she talking about? Is there a baby out there in the forest? He wanted to search but there was no way to know where to begin.

Jay awoke to rocks hitting his window. He opened it up to see Simon, soaking wet.

"It's late, man. What're you doing?"

"Get down here," he said.

Simon told him everything. Jay wanted no part of it.

"This girl is crazy. You thinking about her for two years has made you crazy. She tells you she has a baby in the forest and you want to go find it?"

"Something is wrong with her, man. We need to help."

"Call the cops, then," Jay spit.

"I will once we get the baby out of there, agreed?"

"What if she is dangerous?" asked Jay.

Simon was quiet for a long time before he spoke.

"I don't want to lose her again," he said.

"You may have to give her up. This is going to ruin you." Jay said as he went back into the house. That night, he wondered if Si was already gone.

The next day, Simon arrived on time with soda money from his mother's purse. Sylvia came outside, purse slung over her shoulder with the same hollow look. He embraced her tightly. Sylvia's arms remained at their side. Her scent was strong. She hadn't bathed. Jay was close by with the car. They came up with a plan to let her take Simon to see the baby in the forest and for him to be ready to drive out of there with a kid. There were towels and toys in the backseat.

Simon asked her questions about her parents, her job, anything to take his mind off the idea of stealing a baby away from its mother. Sylvia spoke in a daze.

"Parents saw my baby and left right away. Everyone who's seen him run away. I still think you will," she said before turning her head around towards the highway, flooded with cars.

"No one understands. He's a gift" she said.

She pointed to the dark.

"A gift from the gods."

Simon felt his stomach turn. He wanted to ask what gods.

"You aren't like the others. They always run."

"I think I understand. I just want you to be safe. Even if you don't want to be with me. I want you and the baby to be okay," he said.

He wasn't lying.

She suddenly took his hand and they began to walk along the side of the highway. Jay kept his distance, slowly trailing behind him on side streets until he had to ditch the car and sneak alongside them. Flashlight in hand, Simon kept from asking questions. It felt so good to hold her hand again. Jay followed them well into the night. She held his hand so tight as they went over hills and through dirt paths until they reached the forest. Simon didn't tell Jay about the gun in his coat. The weapon with his father's name was loaded and ready as it had been before.

The girl took them deep into the trees. The highest hills that looked over the city looked so menacing in the dark. Sylvia's white uniform kept Jay from getting lost. Simon stayed silent as his hands began to shiver. He was terrified for the baby, for all of them. Sylvia took them to the caves that sat at the foot of the hills. Jay took off his shoes to keep from breaking branches with his boots. He caught himself on a large branch and decided to pick it up.

Simon stopped at the mouth of the cave. Sylvia tugged at his arm to continue.

"It's okay," she said.

He looked back at the forest. Jay was not there.

"Do you know how to get back?" he asked.

"I've walked this path every night. It's all I know…"

Simon dropped the flashlight to the ground. Jay saw the light and stopped to watch them
enter the cave.

"Don't be afraid," she said.

Sylvia let go of Simon's hand and walked straight into the pitch black. He counted the seconds as he waited. There was a light.

Where did it come from? He looked up to the top of the cave to see an opening. The walls and floors of the stone carried divots filled with green that wrapped and moved together like veins to the bottom where he stood. Where was the light coming from? Simon looked back down to see Sylvia standing before a pool of water.

She called for him.

"Here he is."

Simon was petrified. He took slow steps towards the pool.

"He doesn't stray far from the mouth of the cave."

She spoke so calmly as she looked upon her son. The baby was not human.

The creature sat at the edge of the pool, its skin a mixture of grey and green scales. Its face was covered in eyeballs; all opaque and blinking wildly. It had no arms or legs, only the limbs of snakes that slithered across the stone floor with a sickening sound.

"What is this?"

"The start of something new," she said.

An inhuman sound spilled out from the monstrous child.

The sound shot through the cave. Jay stopped running and dropped the branch.

"What was that?!"

The girl knelt before the creature. She opened her purse as its tentacles wrapped around her legs. The smell wasn't her but the dead creature that she produced and held above its mouth, which opened to reveal spines that stabbed the rotting meat, pulling it into its depths. Simon felt sick. She stood and turned to him.

"They know everything about you. The moment I received the gift, they saw our memories, our lives we lived."

She got closer to him.

"It's how I knew you wouldn't hurt me. It feels your love. I told them you wouldn't be like all the others."

Simon felt for the weapon.

"They can feel your pain. The same pain you have felt all your life; the desire to end it all. You know what I speak of. The feeling that you're a shell, moving in empty circles, a meaningless existence. There is only the void that you feel. The empty space that you cannot run from, the one that has lived within you all your life.”

“Why’re you talking like this?” he whimpered.

“This is the beginning of something special. A shared space with the gods. A blessing from our creator; the ground that holds and keeps us. It chose to bond. To give birth and spread its seed. We have wasted our gift so we are being given another chance.”

“What?”

“Do you remember the story you told me about you going out into the forest? Waiting for the rains, walking in the dirt, trying not to step on the worms?”

Simon began to hear footsteps, but not from the entrance of the cave but from the shadows in front of them. There were dozens of them. Naked. Thin, pale bodies that shared her face. Behind their skin, were strings that moved in time with their legs.

“That’s us,” she said.

“To them, we are the worms.”

Sylvia smiled, she bent down and opened her mouth. From her innards came a sea of the same strings, the same color as the creature. They thrashed and cried out. Simon felt hands on his shoulders. He was surrounded by them. They were stronger than him. He chose to walk.

They led him to the pool and stepped away. Sylvia picked up her child and felt the warm squeeze of its limbs.

Simon looked down to the water. His reflection distorted.

“Receive the gift,” she said.

Jay entered the mouth of the cave to see Simon standing in water. The women backed away as the cave rumbled.

Simon’s head shot back as if it caught a bullet. Jay screamed out. He had seen the tentacle emerge from the pool and recoil back into the water the same second. The women turned to him. From their mouths poured more of the worms. Their thin skin erupted as more pushed through their stomachs.

“Simon?!”

Jay saw him turn back to face him. The weapon was in his hand. Simon pulled the trigger. There was a new hole in his head but something kept his body standing. His eyes went wide.
The worms poured from his mouth to cover the wound.

"Poor daddy," said the girl.

The creature's tentacles shot out. It latched itself to Simon's head and leapt from its mother's arms to his face. She too crumbled to the floor, her body exploding with a thousand strands. Simon was gone. The cave was filled with the worms. Jay screamed and took off for the forest. The light went out from the inside of the cave. Jay blinked his eyes and the sunlight was now outside of the cave.

It was morning? How?

The forest shook with forceful winds. Jay could not remember where he was. He knew the caves, the patch of trees but everything was different now. The path had changed. The sun burned hot and he began to sweat. The trees swayed with the wind that pushed the same heat into his face. He tripped over another branch. When he looked at it, the wood pulsed.

The branch of wood then slithered away. He had no words, no sounds or screams. The ground was hot to the touch. The pathway of cracked branches all began to move with the same rhythm.

The trees, the branches, the wood was alive.

Jay could no longer breathe. He could not find his way out of the forest. There was only the forest. The mouth of the cave was still in sight. It uttered a horrible sound that shook the ground. Trees bent like fingers as the dirt began to rise.

The worms found their way to him.

The creatures entered him any way they could. There was no struggle. Jay's eyes were sealed shut but he could hear the deepest voice, speaking terrifying sounds.

Silence.

Its eyes opened to a glittering blackness.

It took time to stretch and untangle itself.

The sleep weighed heavy on its mind.

It looked down to the rock it had laid upon and felt the happiness of
its children

I grew up with a knife in the chest
my inheritance is a dull blade
placed well enough
for everything to grow around it
the taste of metal is never far
on good days the blade will twist
and people i love are targets
for the weapon forged in me
skin and blood bitter
my face becomes my maker's
a hereditary poison
words taste of fire
seeking nearest wood
i've got a need to burn
to detonate my good thing going
as quick to anger
as she is joy
i am envious
protective of innocent hearts
bite this itching tongue
swallow the blood
i am used to the taste
to closing doors and eating keys
this **"scorched earth signature"**
both gift and lesson

I was supposed to be strong today
but I can't
the weight on this mind
is too heavy right now
to keep from cursing those nearest to the stone
the mouth is bitter with words
I told you I was better than
with all I've forgiven of you
still so much unsettled in me
memory is too good to not replay
the record of our better moments
when we hate each other
forget our progress
and choose venom
I cannot be what I promised
but maybe tomorrow
the sickness will be buried
under the pain of hands clasped so tight
the bones ache

but for now
I dedicate every minute of the day
to easy outs
familiar demons
disrespect
this fatigue is so strong
ask for forgiveness
strength
maybe tomorrow.
I won't sit in corners
crafting theories
for my every misfortune
ignoring every mirror in this house
eyes do nothing now
but seed doubt
when I need this anger the most
to put these words down somewhere
a record of my worst moments
gain another page in the book
of another man
too sick of himself
maybe I will put down the stone
choose to carry my women
place them higher on the mountain
than they were before
maybe tomorrow
today, I am **weak**

From the castle bedroom, the maiden awoke
from a dream of blue faces that never spoke
Her silver eyes turned from the end of the bed
To find her toys climbing to lay at her head
Plush kittens and monkeys with blue and pink fur
Her bear stood guard should an intruder enter
"Dear maiden!" the toys shouted.
"We found the key."
"Thank you," she whispered.
"Now help me be free."
Beyond the bedroom were locked doors and hundreds of halls
With blue paintings, carpets and lights in the walls
Every closet kept dresses, every table had food
They stuffed their faces and bear had some too
The maiden could not rest and began to explore
She lost count of the days wanting to see more
It was then, when she found and opened the door
The moon was so new, never seen before
Was she all alone with just her toys?
Where were all the other moon girls and boys?
A rumble in the distance shook the ground
As a shadow of red made a terrible sound
the dragon's wings covered everything in sight
In its chest was a flower of furious light
"I've been waiting for you," it's voice had boomed
"Why me?" asked the maiden. "What did I do?"
"It's you who I've been waiting to find…
You are not the only one who is the last of their kind."
"The Luna were powerful beyond measure…
Dawn Dragons found you all something to treasure."
"Your Kings and Queens sealed themselves away…
I waited and watched, no others would stay."
"And years have passed, and stay here why?
For the magic and power they had to hide."

The maiden thought of her toys who stood on their own
Did she do that? Because she felt all alone?
"They put a world inside you, girl, and your power is mine."
The bear stepped between them, just in time
The maiden turned and the blue faces were there
She said to them, "I need to save my bear."
"My child, this is real and what it speaks is true…
Your power lies in the dreams our magic gives you."
The spell was done and she remembered the days
Before dragon flame had wiped it away
The castle had no mirrors to show her true face
To remind her it was sealed as a safe place.
"You are the last, go and be, without fear,
But there are so many others who need you here."
The maiden saw the earth and the people below
And every other moon that began to glow
"It's hard to always be so strong…" she said.
"How do I know if this is where I belong?"
"Believe and you will know," said the faces three.
"Dreams give you the power to do more than you see."
The faces were gone with the dragon's roar
A bear knight between his fingers, ready for more
The moon began to glow the maiden's skin blue
The dragon felt its flower break in two
The bear, now free, began to run
Flames erupted and turned a dragon to a Sun
The maiden pushed it far away
The glow of the Sun never faded from that day
The moon was silent as stone, not a peep
The toys could not find her, and went back to sleep
Within the moon, the maiden is still, resting all the same
The dreams of you and I are fuel for the fire of the day
So close your eyes and sleep my dear, for the dawn is coming soon
Your dreams at night will bring new life

To **the maiden in the moon**

my brother is a grown man with the mind of a child
unable to articulate universal angst
to express thoughts and emotions taken for granted
yet excitement often pours from him leading into breaks of dialect
fast moving hands
repeating phrases
all sounds of a forgotten language
buried beneath concrete shackles of disability
the expressions of a lost people
I strain to find the meaning
years ago, I discovered a way for us to connect
we speak in video games
in plumbers and *Pokémon*
snakes under cardboard boxes
with guns blazing, swords clashing
all the furious lights and energy to stir the imagination bringing forth
the bridge
visual media burned as a catalyst to homeschooling
YouTube and Playstation
allowed countless attempts to get the phrasing just right
over and over at all hours of the day, memorizing, recording
understanding emerges making communication slowly possible
my star pupil
valedictorian in the fine arts of *Mortal Kombat, Soul Calibur* and
Marvel vs. Capcom
tinkering with the colors and combinations of clothing for characters
we share opinions through the fashion options of space pirates and
world warriors
the waters of conversation sometimes bubble up into frenzy
"hey jr! look at that! What happened to his head? It exploded!
that's called a fatality…"
choices become preferences, which evolve into favorites
culminating into personality
but some days

there is nothing but brick
regression into the silence of prison walls
where every question you ask is ignored
brother, can you hear me?
"yes"
why are you sad?
"I don't know."
why are you angry?
"I don't know, stop talking please!"
motor skills are hard to recall, eyes staring in directions further away
from a normal life
babies born spared this random collection of genes are molded like
clay from the beginning
into a reflection of its makers and the world around them, for better
or worse
teaching my brother is taking knives to a tree, taking endless
patience and diligence
in guiding the growth of an incomplete work of art
the cost for behavior therapy for children with autism is growing
there are no true government programs to teach him how to survive
And I envy the inner workings of his mind
the fact that he does not yet have to know what it means to worry, or
to dread
or feel the corruption of the world around us
brother, do you know what is happening outside?
"I'm okay! not to worry!"
there is fear of what will happen when or if I go before him
a smile on his face, a laugh that echoes through the rooms of the
house
replaces the discussion we bury and never fully hold
I refuse to die while him becoming institutionalized
remains a possibility
my purpose, more than words on a page that need to be written
to shape the mind of a boy into the strength of a man

press start to begin

there is a pain
that finds its way into the space
between my laughter and my joy
an undeniable ache that finds me
it is constantly seeking
an ear to listen
a conversation of one
its audience running in place
to exit a theater with no doors
sooner or later i stopped
to hear the pitch
it should be easy to ignore
the preachings of a liar
and a thief
i would sit and write
endless pages
promising i wouldn't listen
but i did
no choice but to
when the voice is my own
there is a quiet
i cannot bury
with all my sound
i've been swimming in silences
for too long to curse the whispers
now we converse daily
trade stories in secret
when my body refuses rest
a manuscript of my failures
sits in my phone
collecting all these words
hoping to squeeze a burden
tight enough for it to become
accomplishment

sins of thought are heavy in my chest
tears well within this river bed
ready to burst
when the curve of my lips straightens
keep saying everything is fine
i dream of death now
more than ever
i sit in bathrooms with hands clenched
waiting for the voice to pass
like all things clever
it takes new forms
a small girl with a skull
walks along the streets adjacent
she kicks the leaves
splashes in the biggest puddles
makes piles of the snow
looks my way and turns the corner
sometimes
she has my daughter's face
i hear little bones crack
when she runs to me
new words find her each day
i am humbled by the growth
and wonder if she would do better
without this sunken face
so much good can come from trauma
her strength could surpass mine
such a great story to be told
what perfect example could i be
from the shadows
i feel so welcome in
not wanting the weight of my intention
to repeat the cycle of fear and debt
that makes me

little bones
come and take this pain
i need the will to carry, to commit
but every day i feel less proud
of me
tell me to enjoy this time left
i will say i'm a ticking clock
counting until the parts stop working
or until i choose to use this hammer
leaving marks in my hand
i am a liar and a thief
stealing away my own joy
to bury in the ground
and wait for new dread
everything is fine
when i look in the mirror
and drain the river from my eyes
open my mouth
and invite these poisons
when the house is sleeping
little bones
come and take this pain
i am nothing but a dream
a dancer on the rooftop
the wind no longer cold

Ertrinkender

The fisherman opened his eyes and rose from his bed. The troubles of the day to come had yet to carve their space in his mind. He thought of the sea outside and felt joy. The wooden frame of the bed bent back almost in relief as he got to his feet. His massive frame was hidden by the dark. A winter cap smothered his greased hair parted to the left side. Quietly, he dressed in his usual sweater, trousers and boots. Downstairs in the kitchen, he watched the first rays of sun as he boiled water and grinded beans of coffee. Once done, he tasted the blackened brew. He felt a rush and flooded the cup with cream and sugar. He stopped short of the door when he realized he had forgotten them. He moved back up the stairs and entered the room with reverence. They slept so soundly. He placed a kiss on each of their heads before he made his way back down and out the door. The ship was anchored a mile from the house. He wiped his eyes and raised the anchor from the sand. The sounds of the waves made beautiful music as he readied his nets and his knives. The tide came and pulled the boat away from dry land. As the shore disappeared from sight, the fisherman thought of his wife and child and wept.

Elsewhere, a man took a seat in an office and waited. His trench coat and suit beneath smelled of rust and rain. He studied the paintings of farmland and framed photographs of diplomas on the walls, then went to the papers on the desk. His picture was there, staring up into the ceiling. The door behind him opened and a rough voice cut the silence.

"You are Ritter?"

The man nodded.

"Mayor," he said.

"Dietz, please."

The man's belly pushed across his shoulder as he found his way around the desk to his chair. A dark spot stained his shirt and jacket, both a light blue with pinstripe white.

"My apologies," Ritter reached into his coat for a handkerchief. The man produced one of his own.

"No need. I'm a fat man, as you can tell. It's fine."

He dabbed at the stain on his clothes then at the sweat at the top of his head. The brown spots across his forehead were withered.

"I hoped my invitation would not be ignored. Thank you for coming," he said.

Ritter went back to moving his thumbs in circles.

"You are a detective?"

"I am," said Ritter.

His eyes went back to the folder on the desk. Thick fingers brushed it to the corner.

"You're also a criminal?"

The man waited for a reply, then continued.

"Previously, I should say. I imagine it must be difficult to find work, considering your past. A lot of harassment from my officers? Checking up on you, making sure you don't revert to your old ways?"

Ritter did not flinch.

"I get by," he said.

"Robbery, it says? What happened?"

"Mother was at work. Sisters were hungry," said Ritter.

Dietz cut him off.

"A beautiful story that will get no sympathy here."

There was a long pause between them.

"Do you speak English?"

Ritter nodded.

"Good. You will need that skill, and some others. I won't waste time. There's a reason why you're here. I can't fault any man for trying to survive and feed his family but nevertheless, you are stained."

Ritter looked down to the ground.

"But this is why you are needed. You can place your hands into the dirt my fingers cannot touch. You can go to dark places without a trail leading back to me."

"Where?"

Dietz pointed out the window towards the harbor.

"Along this river, there is a town, far from the jurisdiction of my men. This is where I need you to go. This is where the dirt is. A place beyond the city roads called Liedhaus."

"Never heard of it," said Ritter.

"I don't expect you to. It was built years ago by drifting sailors and carnival folk. It's not a place for tourists. It's a place for escape."

Ritter got to his feet and walked towards the window.

"And who has escaped you?"

Dietz dropped a picture on the desk from his pocket.

"My daughter. Nadja."

Ritter turned from the river and studied the photo. She was beautiful. Long flowing blonde hair wrapped around her head and draped over her neck and shoulders.

"Taken?" he asked.

Dietz shook his head.

"I don't know. We haven't spoken in a long time. She's been pulled to a place far away from me," he said.

"How old is this picture?" asked Ritter.

"Three years ago. She could look completely different now, another reason why I need someone skilled in hiding."

Ritter placed the photo in his jacket pocket.

"And why would she need to hide?" he asked.

"Don't be foolish. I'm not stalking her," muttered Dietz.

Ritter went back to the waters outside.

"If you say so," he said.

His eyes followed the boats slowly cascading down the docks.

"Her mother has passed. Cancer of the liver."

"My condolences," said Ritter.

"Spare me. She was careless and cruel. Guilty of things that are not your business. There's only me now as her ward should her wandering take her somewhere dangerous."

"They might be a tough group to infiltrate. It sounds like they don't take outsiders, especially if they've built their own town to keep people like you and me out."

Dietz ignored him and banged his fist on the desk. Two officers entered.

"There is a boat leaving within the hour. I have a ticket for you.

"We haven't spoken about what's in this for me, sir."

There was a pause.

"What would you want, Herr Ritter? Some money? Your records expunged? A clean slate and my fine gentlemen off your back? I figured you to be the type of man to not ask for favors when given a task."

Ritter said nothing.

"Say no more. I will give you those things. Hopefully your affairs are somewhat in order?"

Ritter looked at the men. Both gripped their guns.

"Would you let me leave if they weren't?" he asked.

Dietz smiled.

"No, I wouldn't," he said.

The officers took Ritter by the arms. One reached into his coat pocket. Ritter recoiled but the grip on his arm was joined with a nightstick to his back.

"Liedhaus is a place far off the grid," said Dietz.

"There are no roads and there are no lines of communication."

The officer who searched Ritter pulled out his phone and dropped it on the table.

"What should I do if there is an emergency?" asked Ritter.

"You've been to prison, right? You should be able to take care of yourself. I will be your only communication. I expect an update in three days. Should there be any delay, consider our deal rescinded. There will be a carrier there to bring your letters."

"Do you trust the post?" asked Ritter.

"Letters can be burned. Electronic words last forever," said Dietz.

The men escorted him from the office. Ritter did not struggle. It would only make it worse. Dietz's voice called out from behind him as they approached the stairwell.

"Don't return without her," he said.

Ritter had already decided that he wouldn't. Two years under Dietz's thumb was enough. He wasn't making enough money and had to break away. He needed to start fresh. The ride down the river was spent away from the eyes of the boatman. His voice was too shrill. Ritter heard the stories about the wrecked vessels at the bottom of the river. It hurt his ears every time he broke into song but he managed to return a smile when he remembered to. The canals stretched out like fingers in all directions. He looked deep into the waves and watched the ripples cut across his reflection. So easy to jump in, he thought. Ritter had never learned how to swim.

The fear had gripped his veins when he was a boy and never let go. His father threw him into the water. It was meant for him to learn. Ritter never understood why. It had only damaged him. His older sister dove in to save him after his father stopped counting and turned his back. His heart stopped for a minute before he began coughing up water. The fever broke a week later. He could hear the cries of the girls long after he had healed. Their screams would come in his sleep; shrill cries and then water. Ritter dreamed of drowning more than anything else. The air in his lungs would be gone and his mouth would fill with liquid. His arms would cease to move and his body became stone. Ritter's eyes remained open as he sank to the bottom. When he woke, the bed would be covered in sweat.

He told himself he would find the girl, bring her to Dietz and then he would be gone. The trip to Liedhaus took until the morning. The boatman stopped for beer and a meal at an alehouse along the river bank. Ritter paid him for the food and tipped him once they arrived at shore. A storm had come and buried the sun with clouds that stained the sky and earth a dark blue. There were no other boats besides the one that carried him. The ground was soaked by vicious rain. Ritter's bag was soaking wet before he left the dock. The town and harbor that Dietz had spoken of looked mostly abandoned and was falling apart. Two sailors stood in the distance with their hands hidden. The rotting wood bent beneath his feet as he approached the town.

Liedhaus truly was built from nothing. There was a town square with bars and storefronts all made from the same weathered lumber. Rope and pieces of broken ships filled the gaps in the buildings where they ran out of materials. Small, quaint houses were lined in rows of five facing north and south. Buildings with painted signs, including ones that said "Bar", "Mail" and a small shop that simply said "Meat" ran east and west. Ritter thought about counting the money in his pocket but kept his hands in his coat as he passed the sailors. He met eyes with them and nodded his head.

"Staying for a while?" asked one.

"For a few nights, if there's room," said Ritter.

A sailor stepped in his way.

"We're full here, friend," he said.

Ritter stopped and motioned towards the bar.

"I've got enough for at least a bottle," said Ritter.

The second sailor approached and pulled a knife from his pocket.

"We don't like to share," he said.

Ritter's eyes pointed down. The sailor looked to see the barrel of a revolver poking through his coat and pointed at his groin.

"I insist," said Ritter.

The sailors looked at each other and then laughed.

"I think you will do just fine," said the first.

Ritter was led down the street.

"What brings you here?" asked the second.

"Looking for someone," said Ritter.

The first sailor pointed towards the houses.

"Not many places to look," he said.

"Small group, close knit," said the second.

Ritter knew what they meant. They weren't going to give up information easily. Whoever wanted to be missing went there to stay that way.

The door to the bar swung open. Two dim lights in the back corners kept them from knocking over chairs and tables. The men greeted each other with glances. Ritter wondered if they had given every new visitor the same treatment. The rain outside battered the roof and drowned out the music coming from the jukebox. There were others in the room. The other figures did not speak. Ritter could see them from the corner of his eye. No food or drink on their tables. They could have been waiting out the rain, he thought. They could also have been waiting to greet their newest visitor should they say the wrong thing.

The bartender lit a candle and placed it at Ritter's spot. Shadows laced the walls with new rising shapes as they took their seats. He ordered a bottle of their strongest and let the sailors take their share.

"How long will you be here, friend?" asked the bartender.

Ritter took a moment to choose his words.

"As long as I can," he said.

The bartender shook his head.

"How did you hear about this place?" he asked.

"The boatman sang a song about it, leaving the city," said Ritter.

The bartender stopped cleaning a glass and leaned forward.

"We know the boatman. They don't bring people here unless they ask to be brought here. Any cops behind you?" he asked.

The sailors got quiet.

"No, sir," said Ritter.

"We don't like Police here," the first sailor shouted.

They had finished the bottle already.

"We also don't like people making up stories. We're all friends here. Are you a policeman? You wouldn't lie to us, would you?" asked the second.

Another test, he thought. Ritter kept his face the same.

"Just tired is all," he said.

"Looking for a place to sleep?" asked the bartender.

Ritter nodded.

"Some rooms to the East. Mention Frederick. Discount per night on me. You're welcome. Say nothing else."

"What's out here for entertainment?" asked Ritter.

The sailors laughed. The bartender's face straightened.

"The Raven House. Go west. Good company there," he said.

Ritter thanked him for the bottle.

"Don't push your luck," said the bartender.

The second sailor placed a hand on his back and blew out the candle.

"There's eyes all about you. We appreciate the drink but don't come here thinking you're safe. No one comes here for that," said the second.

"Outsiders come here to take what we have. You won't be doing any of that now, will you?" asked the first.

Ritter found himself surrounded. A deep voice bellowed from another corner that cut through every other sound.

"A terrible way to greet a fellow traveler," it said.

The sailors slinked away as the bartender looked up at the size of the man and began to quickly light another candle.

"See how they run when face to face with a man they know good and well?"

Ritter felt a massive hand on his shoulder.

"Scare tactics do nothing to find the truth of a stranger. You find it in their eyes."

The voice had been coming from the body of a giant. The man was nearly seven feet tall. His tattered clothes and wrinkled face told a story. He was a fisherman. His large, calloused hand stuck out.

"Gern," said the fisherman.

The handshake was overpowering. Gern took a seat next to him and pointed to the wood of the bar. A mug of beer was there in seconds. His face went from serious back to a smile just as quickly.

"They always ask me to come and examine who steps off a boat. I tell them they're insane. It's raining. You're wet and weary."

Gern downed half the beer and turned back to him.

"If you're looking to make trouble, you wouldn't do it right off the boat, right? You would wait until at least the morning, no?"

Ritter nodded. The fisherman motioned to the bartender to make sure they were all in agreement. He pulled a toothpick from his pocket and began to dig into his teeth.

"Now, who are you looking for?" asked Gern.

He turned and looked into Ritter's eyes. Even the toothpick was bigger than normal.

"For my sister," he said.

"Got a picture?" asked Gern.

Ritter took the photo of Nadja from his pocket and showed it to him. The fisherman leaned forward. He looked at Ritter and back to the photo.

"Name?"

"Nadja," said Ritter.

"No doubt a man looking for his family is not in the mood to cause problems for strangers. So here's what I say; the Raven House is a place for the wrong kind of people. I suggest you keep your distance. They won't take care of you, even if you take care of them. Show respect to the town. Don't hurt my friends. Do you understand?"

Ritter understood.

"Everyone here is civil. Don't worry about these fools. They're worried about letting the wrong kind into our little paradise."

Gern stabbed at his tooth again with his massive pick.

"There are no monsters here. Unless you consider me," he said.

The fisherman said goodbye to Ritter and waved at the bartender before sauntering out into the storm. The other bodies hidden in the shadows got up and went home as well. He looked back to the bartender, who handed him a pamphlet. He would look at it later. Ritter left the tavern and headed north to a sign of red painted letters.

"Hotel."

He laughed. No fancy name for anything usual. Bar. Hotel. Meat. But then some place called the Raven House? Ritter checked in with the name given and laid down in his wet clothes. The storm carried on through the night. After a few hours, he got to his feet and undressed. He forgot to check the pillows and sheets for bugs. Too late now, he thought. Even wrapped up, the blanket was not enough to warm him. Ritter fell into an ugly sleep as he thought again of water filling his lungs. The pressure in his chest was heavy. The morning hit him like a sharp blow to the side of his head. His body did not rest. Ritter put on his spare clothes and visited the town square to ask around about Nadja. The carnival folk that Dietz mentioned were nowhere to be found. The town seemed hollow and distant.

The locals who remained did not speak much on who had come through and left their small corner of the world. The people of Liedhaus were all about peace and quiet. They shrugged off his questions about Nadja and kept on about farming, and how dreadful life in the cities were before they heard of this place. Some of them were sick and asked Ritter to keep his distance. Many of them came from the same place as he; looking for a way to carve a life out from the thumb of institutions he knew all too well, including the one who had sent him.

No one knew who Nadja was. No one had seen her around in town. When asked about the Raven House, Ritter was told the same thing.

"Open at sundown. Knock five times."

Ritter made his way back to his room. He waited for the night. He ate some bread before trying to nap and hopefully get his strength back. When he first woke, he turned his attention to the pamphlet from Frederick the night before. A sketch of women with wings for arms and heads of birds adorned the cover. He studied it between fits of sleep until the dark had come. Inside the book was a poem and map with directions made in wonderful handwriting to help lead those curious to the Raven House. Was it possible Dietz's child turned to the night to survive? The ones who built houses out here were not carnival folk, he thought. That night, Ritter found it with ease.

The house looked to be painted a thick black. Upon closer inspection, Ritter found that the texture wasn't of paint, but feathers. The entire house was covered in them, carefully glued to the wood. The feathers created a fine tapestry that sealed the house off from the outside world. A purple light emanated from behind the sea of black that covered the windows. A knock on the door was answered by a raven with the legs of a woman.

The purple light shot out and cut the dark behind them. The raven's body was hidden by her wings.

"Do you know what you're looking for?" it asked.

"Good conversation, maybe?" asked Ritter.

The raven opened her wings to reveal only skin. She was indeed a woman.

"You will find that and more," she said.

Ritter followed her inside. The house within was just as feathered as the outside. Birds with human legs stalked the living and dining rooms. Guests were seated and entertained. Each man caressed the wings of their hostess. Not just ravens were houses here, but birds of all kinds moved through the rooms. He counted the creatures; a wren, a sparrow and dove. Ritter was escorted to a red velvet kitchen. The scent of seasoned pork overwhelmed his senses. He hadn't eaten enough. The smell was intoxicating. A man stepped into the room. His face was hideously scarred.

"Hungry?" asked the man.

"Starving," said Ritter.

The raven disappeared back into the living room. Ritter looked back to see a hand extended.

"William," said the scarred man.

"A pleasure," Ritter replied.

He looked in all directions, unsure of what to think. A gurgling began in the pit of his stomach.

"Questions?" William began.

"What is this?" asked Ritter.

"We're the welcoming committee."

Ritter did not notice that William kept his grip on his hand until then.

"How many others have tried to scare you off since your arrival?"

"Nearly everyone," said Ritter.

The scarred man then pulled him closer.

"Well, that's a relief because I'm a much better host than intimidator," he laughed and released his grip.

"What are you hosting, exactly?" asked Ritter.

"My friend, we are the only entertainment here in Liedhaus. This was the first house built upon this soil once the deed was purchased."

"You own this land?"

"The community owns the land. I couldn't be the face of our group. Can't you tell?"

"I didn't mean to..." said Ritter.

William led him back into the makeshift parlor.

"You did nothing. This house is of my design. The women here are all artists. We provide services of comfort to those who need a taste of the arts. Did you like the pamphlet?" asked William.

"Beautiful writing," said Ritter.

"You get only the best here, good sir."

William pointed to the birds of the Raven House, each had an older man hanging on their every word.

"So you know, our services are divvied by coin. You can have a song, a poem, a dance. It costs a little bit more to take one home," said William.

Ritter raised an eyebrow and began to understand.

"The birds, as you say, do not show their faces here?" he asked.

"Anonymity is key to a place like this, friend. Some of the town look down on us, turn their noses up at what we do. Some of the worst offenders were my best customers."

Ritter put pieces together about what may have happened to Nadja.

"Have any of your birds ever fallen in love and run off with a customer?" he asked.

William took him to a seat away from the others. He was intrigued.

"Are you looking for one in particular?" he asked.

Ritter showed the picture.

William studied the photo, much like the fisherman did. It was the look of familiarity. Ritter hoped he would learn something.

"Lovely young woman. Family?"

Ritter nodded.

"Are you Police?" asked William.

"Everyone has asked me that. I'm not. I'm just trying to find her. It's been years. I worry that something terrible has happened. This town, this place is all I have to go on," said Ritter.

He changed his face to show some desperation.

"As much as my tongue wishes to reveal information that may help you on your journey, my principals are strong. I cannot tell you where she has gone. But I would like to tell you the story of my face. Would you like to hear it?"

"Sure," said Ritter.

"Many years ago, I was a stowaway on a ship moving across the Atlantic from one side of the world to the other. This was how I survived. A failed student with little education was not going to get far without the water as a guide. There was a horrible crash. The ship was pulled away from the path and could not regain control."

"So many men died that night. I thought that I would join them at the bottom. I did not have the energy to get to shore. Something had found me, however. After I lost consciousness, I was carried to an island, the inhabitants of which were not human. They were something different; a mixture of animal and man. It was a tribe, you know. They wore the heads of the animals they hunted. I woke to screaming boar heads. They were covered in blood and ravenous. I could still see their teeth behind the open mouths of their masks. I didn't speak their language. They did not listen to my cries. I was too sick to eat, as well. They were complete savages."

"Did you run?" asked Ritter.

"I didn't. I couldn't. They grew tired of my noise and tied me to a tree. I was near death and delirious as it was, so I was prepared for being made a feast of. Instead, they decided to show me their crown."

"Crown?" Ritter was confused.

"It was their instrument. A perfect design, really. Within the crown of branches, were the pointy ends, you see."

William's hands demonstrated how the crown had worked.

"The moment you feel the ends, they push down and you are their king for the night."

With a snap of William's fingers, the dove had produced a mixed drink. She placed it carefully into Ritter's hand.

"The crown was pushed down far enough so it would not come off. Soon after, they lit a fire at the top of my head," continued William.

Ritter was speechless.

"The fire scorched the wood. It traveled down and burned my skin like kindling. I don't have to tell you how much it hurt. There isn't a word I could use to describe it justly."

Ritter caught himself checking the glass. The drink was strong.

"They found me the next day. The folds of my cheeks had poured off. My forehead was gone but lucky for me, the rain had come and doused their fire. The tribe slowly put me back together. I had lived through their ceremony. It was only then that they decided to free me."

"I'm glad that they did," Ritter said.

The dove brought another glass, a rye whiskey, its top still aflame. William doused the fire and toasted to him.

"Why do you think I told you this story?"

"I have no idea," said Ritter.

"My scars are proof of strength. I wear this melted face with honor. So many newcomers to the Raven House are afraid of me. You've shown me respect by looking into my eyes. You also checked the glass, which shows you are not as much a fool as the people here say you are."

Ritter laughed. The word was already getting out about him. Time was running out.

"Feel free to stare at my scars and even touch them, if you wish."

"No, thank you," Ritter stuttered.

"All this is meant to say, that you are welcome in the Raven House, friend. After my time on the island with the tribe, I'm used to living underneath 'alphas'," said William.

Ritter wondered what he meant by that.

"I appreciate that. But is there any information you can give me to help me find my sister?" he asked.

William took a long drink from the glass.

"I've shared my story and my pain with you. I can only hope you believe me to be a man of honor. In doing so, I hope I can expect the same," he said.

Ritter agreed.

"Is she really your sister?"

Maybe the drink was stronger than he thought, but there was no hesitation.

"She's not," said Ritter.

"And you are with the Police?" asked William.

"I am not. I find missing people. This is not a paying gig. Forced by the family. I've been told not to return to my city without her."

William finished his drink and held his glass above his head. The dove swooped in to retrieve the glass. Behind her wing was another, topped off.

"I figured as much. I have known enough liars and have read their faces like good stories. Some of the best liars live here on this land. This girl's family must have a tight grip on your life, eh? Connections with all the right people? Enough to make your life difficult?"

Ritter nodded.

William stood up. He quickly finished his whiskey and placed it on the table.

"I wish you good luck on your journey, friend. Please take care in Liedhaus. Whenever you're ready for a companion, don't hesitate to approach a bird and make your request."

He placed a single coin on the table and walked away. Ritter took the coin and pocketed it. He finished his drink and turned to survey the parlor. The raven stood in the corner. She was watching him. Was she waiting? He raised his hand. The bird opened her wings again and approached. Ritter tried to look away but failed.

"Good evening," said the raven.

"I'd like to make a request," said Ritter.

The raven took a seat on his lap. Her pale skin looked white as milk beneath her cape of feathers.

"I would like to hear a song, please."

Ritter reached in his pocket for extra euros. The raven stopped him.

"A song is only a coin," she said.

The raven took the coin from his pocket and leaned back against Ritter. He could feel the weight of the wings and the head of the bird as she moved in circles.

"Tell me what you want to hear," she whispered.

Ritter pulled the picture from his pocket and placed it on her stomach.

"Can you sing me a song about this girl?" he asked.

The raven sat up and turned to face Ritter. She brought her wings up and draped them over his shoulders.

"The girl was a raven before me," she began.

"She sings and dances like me. Sometimes, she would go home with our guests and return in the morning."

"When did you see her last?" asked Ritter.

"Weeks ago. She left with a man."

"Can you tell me who it was?" Ritter whispered back.

"The fisherman," said the raven.

He was not surprised. Still, a hole began to grow in his stomach.

The raven pulled up her mask enough for her lips to kiss his cheek. She could tell he was afraid of the fisherman, too.

"Do you think something bad happened to her?" asked Ritter.

"Liedhaus is a shadow of its old days. The carnival folk are gone, except for William. He stayed to make sure we felt safe, that we weren't hurt. Bad things still happen all the time. Once he is gone, these birds will fly."

The raven got to her feet. Her hand lingered on his chest.

"Maybe you should fly too, while you still have wings to carry you."

She wrapped herself in her wings and moved to another customer. Ritter got to his feet and made for the exit.

William saluted him as he stepped outside. The drink from the Raven House held a tight grip on him. Something big was suddenly in the way of the street. Ritter fell to the ground instantly. A shadow blocked out the light of the moon. Ritter found himself looking up at the fisherman.

"You don't listen, do you?" asked Gern.

He looked Ritter up and down from head to toe as he got to his feet. The fisherman sneered and chuckled.

"You went to the place I told you not to. Curiosity is a curse," he said.

Ritter stepped back and put his hands up.

"It's been a long day with no progress," he said.

"Hey, it's your money to waste! I told you not to go. There's nothing in there but freaks and little girls who lie and steal."

The fisherman smelled of booze as well. He pulled his toothpick from his pocket and dug it into his teeth again.

"Go to bed, kid. You smell terrible," he said.

Gern spat out something dark and brown next to Ritter's shoe and swaggered off into the darkness. Ritter looked down at the dirt and waited a long time before he tried to get to his feet. He felt a hand on his shoulder. It was William.

"On your feet, my friend," he said.

Ritter got up and swept the dirt from his suit.

"Is it a coincidence that he was here as soon as I was leaving?" he asked.

"As I said. I'm used to living underneath 'alphas'. Nothing that happens here is coincidence," said William.

The raven was onto something. William had a role to play in town. He wouldn't upset their delicate balance. There was still the question of proof. Ritter laid in his bed and stared a hole into the ceiling. His thoughts were troubled now with more than just the water. In the morning, there was a letter that was slipped beneath his door. Ritter opened it to find directions to a house. Did William do this? Outside, the soil had finally dried from the rains the night he had arrived. His footsteps sounded solid as he followed the note. The directions had taken him back to the dock where he landed but he followed the shore as instructed.

There was a small beach almost hidden from the broken wood harbor and piecemeal homes that sat a few miles away. The house was quaint and simple; white painted brick and a brown wooden roof. Ritter wondered if Gern had built his home away from the others. It was built from good materials, no recycled pieces of wrecked ship or feathers in sight. There were prints in the sand of both foot and anchor. The fisherman was gone. Now was the time to search the house. Ritter looked to the last line of the note.

"Side door, window to the right."

There was a small staircase that led up from the white sand to the side of the house. The side door itself was locked tight, as expected. There was no key beneath the rug outside. Two windows, one locked and one with an open sill were there next to the locked door. He asked himself why the window was left open. It was then when he heard a voice, coming from upstairs. He approached the stairs. The voice was not in pain. It was a beautiful sound.

She was singing.

He had slipped off his shoes to avoid footprints.Pictures of Gern holding massive fish and laughing maniacally decorated the walls. He looked behind each door to find the source of the song. Behind the notes, he heard the calm splashing of water. The voice came not from the bathroom but another bedroom. Ritter opened the bedroom door and saw a large tank of water. The blankets and sheets that covered the top were thrown to the floor. Inside the glass tank was a woman with no legs. Instead of legs, she had the tail of a fish.

Ritter was frozen. Her hair was a wild mess of blonde. She had the bluest eyes he had ever seen. The woman put a finger to her lips. Beside her, floating in the water, was a young boy with the same tail. The boy was fast asleep. The woman swam up to the edge of the tank.

"Hello," she said.

"Uh, good day...Ma'am," said Ritter.

"Lorelei," she said.

"I'm sorry?"

"My name is Lorelei."

"Ritter," he said.

She motioned to the sleeping child behind her.

"Try not to wake him. He's been having nightmares."

Ritter looked at the boy and began to put the pieces together.

"He won't be back until tonight."

Ritter hesitated, then checked the hallway to make sure no one was there.

"You're looking for the girl, yes?"

"I'm sorry?" he stammered.

"It's true. She's not the only one."

Ritter felt a chill run through him. William was right about him, as was the raven. Gern had some kind of hold over everyone. Was he afraid of them finding this out?

"There's so many others like her, resting in pieces at the bottom of the water," she said.

"Why are you telling me this?" he asked.

"Because we are prisoners," she said.

"Did you help him?" he asked.

"I only eat what I am fed," said Lorelei.

Ritter's heart sank. So much for the question of proof.

"It's so lonely here. I've never had the chance to entertain someone before. I can barely remember the feel of the sea outside. This water is so cold," said Lorelei.

"How long have you been here?" asked Ritter.

"Since the day I found him floating in the water. When he woke up, he told me he heard my song and had to find me. His arms were so strong, I could not get free. He carried me to another man's ship. He put his hands around his neck and made him go to sleep. I was brought here. He kept the man's ship, built a home for us and a tank for me."

"I'm so sorry," said Ritter.

He couldn't help but fall deeper into her bluest eyes.

"All that matters is that you're here now," she said.

Lorelei put her hand out.

"Can you touch me?" she asked.

Ritter felt his heart skip. She smiled and he could see her teeth. Each one was sharpened, filed almost like fangs. Still, he approached and reached out. Lorelei grabbed his hand and put it to her cheek.

"You're so warm, Ritter," she said.

His heart almost stopped when she said his name. Her touch loosened his shoulders.

"You'll help us, won't you?" asked Lorelei.

Ritter felt a sting that brought his attention back to his hand. She has bitten his finger. His body made a strange new shiver.

"You can save us," she whispered.

Lorelei kissed the wound she made and licked it clean.

"Can I search the house?" he asked.

"You won't find anything. He's too smart to leave a trace," she said.

Ritter kept quiet. Was this creature stolen from the sea? Was Gern ruling over the people in Liedhaus through fear?

"You'll come back tomorrow, won't you?" asked Lorelei.

"Does your husband ever stay home?" Ritter whispered.

She shook her head.

"He only returns to sleep and to feed us. This room is all we've seen for years," she said.

Ritter said goodbye and slowly crept back out of the house. He walked back down the shore to his room as he stared at the wound on his hand. There was an itch that came from the holes her teeth made. He put his tongue on them when they began to bleed again, and it tasted sweet.

He climbed into his bed and stayed there. Ritter did not think of the water like before. The voice of the woman and her song flooded his heart with something new. It felt like hope. In the morning, Ritter crafted his first letter to Dietz. He took time to craft a story that would keep the facade intact. Much like William, he understood the need for balance. Ritter needed time to understand what had happened and what he now felt.

Every three days, Ritter would craft a letter over breakfast to take to the postman. He kept his face as somber and overworked as the letters implied. The sealed windows filled the single room with dust that lined every corner and surface within. The man said nothing every time. Ritter still dropped extra coins for his troubles. His visits to Lorelei became frequent. It brought him happiness. Ritter was introduced to her son, Finn. He was a happy boy who acted like he knew nothing of his father. Maybe it was true. Still, Ritter played with him while Lorelei brushed her hair and told stories of life beneath the sea; diving deep to gather food for the other maidens, watching boats ride the waves from underneath, sometimes seeing the vessels topple over and seeing the men struggle to get to safety.

To Ritter, it all sounded like a fairytale. He wanted so badly not to be terrified of the water. Lorelei had warned Finn to not speak of their new friend who came to visit. Most days, she would sing a song to put him to sleep to give her and Ritter time alone.

Her kiss was electric.

Ritter would tell her of his own nightmares, where they began and how often he would wake in terror. She would pull him close to sing in his ear and then drown him in her kiss. The bites on his lips and neck were more difficult to conceal. The sweetness that poured from his wounds like a sap continued. It tasted like the nectar from the vines of a tree. He remembered how he would cut and drink from the vines of the trees behind his home. Ritter felt himself falling for Lorelei, but the more he let the feeling overtake him, there was fear of reprisal from not only Gern, but Dietz as well. Between their time together, Ritter studied the fisherman. Gern's routine consisted of gathering fish and oddities to sell, followed by nights of heavy drinking and assaulting people in town. Ritter kept his distance and avoided the night. He never went back to the Raven House. A part of him knew that seeing Lorelei had crossed a line he could not return from. He was on his own.

On the morning of the ninth day, Ritter opened his eyes and felt the crushing weight again. For the first time in days, he was again afraid of the water. Lorelei's song did not lull him to sleep. Her voice seemed to pull him deeper than before. Ritter tossed and turned in bed and felt a growing pain in his throat. He wrote another report to Dietz that spoke of another false lead for the location of Nadja, another dead end in his investigation. He asked for more time but he knew that something had to change.

Ritter opened the door to his room and found a knife stuck in the wood. Carefully, he pulled it out and pocketed the weapon. He made his way out and snuck to the postman to drop the letter. There was one for him this time. Ritter dropped a few coins on the counter and wiped the dust from his sleeve. Inside was a response from Dietz.

"Spending all your time in another man's bed will get you hurt," it said.

Ritter took the paper and crumpled it. Dietz had been lying to him all along. Outside the door were two men in trenchcoats. Their eyes were hidden behind sunglasses. Ritter only thought of Lorelei. The men motioned for the boat at the edge of the harbor. Ritter thought of the revolver and the dagger. He decided to go with them. They took the long road through the center of Liedhaus. Those in the square saw them and said nothing. Ritter kept his eyes down until he looked up to see William. He was there, bags of fruit and wine in hand, still dressed in his velvet suit. The scarred man nodded his head and suddenly walked in front Dietz's men, cutting them off from the boats.

"Gentlemen please," said William.

"Before you go, perhaps I could offer you a free visit to the Raven House?"

One of Dietz's men responded only with a bullet to the leg. William fell to the ground, wounded but not finished. Ritter snuck away and cut a corner behind a house. Gern was there, staring at him and smiling. The fisherman blocked his path to the field he took to visit Lorelei away from the eyes of the townspeople. Ritter bumped into his chest. Gern swatted him to the ground.

"Stupid punk," he said.

Ritter got up and dusted himself off.

"Those men are for you, yeah? Do me a favor and go with them. Get out of here so I don't have to hurt you," said Gern.

The fisherman advanced on Ritter. Another gunshot echoed out, followed by distant screams.

"What's that on your neck, son?" he asked.

Ritter held out the toothpick from Gern's pocket, then he showed him the dagger left on his door.

"This is from her, am I right?" he asked.

"So you think you know me now?" Gern opened his shirt to reveal more of the same marks on his chest and neck.

"You think you're the only one? Do you think you're special?" asked Gern.

"I know what you've done. You're an animal. Down to gnawing on the bone of your victims. I've seen not just to this town, but to Nadja, and Lorelei and your boy Finn, too," said Ritter.

"Don't speak their names to me!" Gern screamed out. The sound curdled Ritter's blood. He had to get away from him.

"I told you there were no monsters here, boy. Monsters come from the sea," said the fisherman.

Ritter went to run. Gern was faster. His grip was inescapable. The dagger was enough to slip between his fingers and open his hand up. Ritter went down the same alley and was greeted by Dietz's men with guns drawn. They were standing over William. His eyes were still open, facing the sun. He tossed them the bone and made for the shoreline. The men went to fire but Gern was there. He pulled the guns from their hands and then pulled the bones out from their joints.

"He's mine!"

The new screams were horrifying. Ritter did not turn back to see what he had done. The boatman quickly pulled away from shore and went back down the river. There were furious noises behind him. Gern called out over and over.

"Where are you going now? I left your friends alive! You solved your little mystery, huh? Mission accomplished!"

Ritter kept going until he saw the house. The boat was there, anchor down. He kicked the door open and made his way upstairs to Lorelei's room. She was asleep when he entered. Ritter bashed his fist against the tank.

"He's here. He knows and he's coming," he whispered.

Lorelei opened her eyes. Finn still lay asleep, turning in the water. Her eyes turned to terror and she backed away to the other side of the tank. Gern took Ritter up with one hand and broke the wall with his body.

"You think you know anything about love, boy?!" hollered Gern.

He slammed his hand against the tank so hard, the glass had cracked. Ritter went for the revolver.

Before he could pull the trigger, Gern slapped it from his hand. A large fist cracked his teeth. Ritter spit out blood and slowly crawled out to the hallway.

Gern placed a kick into his ribs that sent him down the stairs to the floor.

"It was her song that led me to the rocks. It was what she did for fun, you idiot. And now, you think you're going to save her from me?"

Gern stood on Ritter's chest. He screamed out and felt something crack beneath his skin.

"You fed them your victims. You're the monster."

Ritter could barely speak.

"I kept them safe. Once I knew I was going to be a father, I knew I had to protect them anyway I could. You know she could have left any time she wanted, right? Even before the boy was born," said Gern.

The fisherman kneeled down on Ritter's chest. He felt the air leave his lungs.

"She's a legend. Things like her are not supposed to be real. When I came home, the others told stories of creatures like her, warning us about their seductive song. What do you think would happen if those people outside found out about her? About my boy? Even if she fell out of love...with me, I still took care of them."

Gern knelt down even closer to Ritter's ear.

"You think you're the first man she's called here with her voice?"

Ritter looked into his eyes.

"There's no need for words...not anymore," said Gern.

"No matter what happens, there'll be another. Whatever she told you, it's a lie. Her kiss will not give you what you want. If you step into that water, you'll drown, like any man."

He placed his hand over Ritter's mouth.

"Sleep and dream of the sea. It's the only way you'll see it like she promised," he said.

The frying pan came from nowhere and crashed on the fisherman's head. Lorelei was there, struggling to sit upright and breathe while holding the weapon. Gern got to his feet and put his hands around her neck. Ritter sat up and saw the boy. He was holding the pan now.

A single shot to the skull was not enough to fell the giant

He raised the pan and brought it down on his father's head again and again. Lorelei's bluest eyes rolled back into her head.

Ritter took the pan from the boy and brought down the iron as hard as he could on the back of the fisherman's head.

The massive man fell face first and was still. Ritter and Lorelei embraced. She wanted to thank him but both mother and child were out of breath. Ritter carried them to the shore and watched them breathe in the air he couldn't.

He felt the bones pressing against his skin and crumpled in pain. He turned to the land and saw more men approaching the house.

The back door smashed open. It was Gern. His eyes were full of rage. There was no going back to land.

Lorelei called his name. He didn't answer.

"Was he telling the truth?" asked Ritter.

She looked confused.

"What do you mean?" she asked.

"Gern...Was he lying? Were there others before me?"

Lorelei said nothing.

"You sang to me every night. You said it would change me."

She looked back at her son and then to Ritter.

"Take my hand, love," she said.

Ritter felt a pain in his chest.

She said love. Her hand was outstretched. He crawled to her and held her hand. Lorelei caressed his head and sang the song that filled his heart with joy every night.

"Do you love me?" she asked.

The sounds of the world he knew were furious behind him.

"Yes," he said.

"Then have faith in me," said Lorelei.

She slowly returned to the water. He watched her lower her head into the water and open her mouth. Lorelei took the deepest breath.

Ritter walked out into the blue and watched them fall back into the waves, their hands called him forward.

A question of faith? That's all it was?

Slowly, the water came up to his legs, his chest and finally his neck. The woman moved so gracefully. The gleam of the sun illuminated everything around him.

The sounds of the waves had calmed and became almost welcoming. Ritter kept walking until the sea had claimed him.

Stella Moon Weiss turned five years old the day she first saw the shadows in her bedroom hallway move. A bladder full of milk, birthday cookies and cake drove her from sleep to careful steps to the bathroom. Her heart froze as wood creaked from some unknown corner. From the closet at the end of the second floor poured black liquid from the bottom of the door. Shapes crawled forward from the puddle that grew larger. They were emptied slow from an unseen glass big enough to drown her in. Her screams cut through the rooms of the house. As soon as the hallway light came on, both the puddle and the arms that pulled from it were gone.

Both mother and father comforted her with a passing caress of her hair, a brilliant platinum blonde. She would find safety in their arms until her body lost the fight to welcome the sun and sweetly collapsed. For months, they told her to not be afraid of the dark. She wanted to be brave, but they had not seen what she had; something that moved against the presence of light, a special black that poured from the darkness, sometimes as fingers, or arms, even a half formed face with lips that mumbled horrible nothings.

The days piled atop one another until they felt like stone. Their attempts to console began to wane as repetition increased. Stella soon turned six, then seven. Her mania increased as the stories of other children her age began to vanish in the night. There was talk of a man, draped in dark who would come to steal the children away. She knew better than the newspapers and the whispers of the old ladies at bus stops and corner stores.

The children at school spoke of the vanishings as well. They all carried dull and listless faces. She spent what felt like endless hours of endless days with them. Each made their own stories to disappear into the ether as the words of the adults. Nothing was proven. But Stella had seen the shadows move. She had seen what others could not. A cute boy by the name of Philip had shared his same dreams of moving dark arms and they formed a bond. Play dates in the park and bike rides through the neighborhood they had only recently realized they shared had created a shield from the menace that pressed against their bedroom doors.

One day, Phillip took his webcam and left it on during the night. His laptop was set to record any event that would take place in the room. Stella had asked to watch it with him. The next day, he showed her the footage. A lurching black covered the room, and soon the floor, the wall, the windows, the camera itself. They gripped each other tightly in the playground as the other children laughed and screamed. The darkness covered the lens of the camera, but the few seconds of footage left showed nothing but the chattering of endless teeth, gnashing and gnawing, ravenous for any food pulled beneath the black.

There was no webcam anymore, he told her. From then on, she could not keep her silence. Her parents were forced to act by the wishes of the schoolmasters. Therapy and medications dulled her senses and helped her focus on assignments and chores. Time passed differently. Within a few weeks, Phillip had stopped trying to get her attention. Days later, he too was claimed by the same invisible force churned up by the public. Doctors stored her accounts, her illustrations of the blackness and submitted them to psychiatric study. Phillip was gone, laptop included. The results of her study came back inconclusive. With the snap of their fingers, all the trouble was written off, considered another overactive imagination. Stella learned that she would need to wear a mask that they created if she was to carry on.

She hadn't forgotten any of it. In time, she learned to use the light against her enemy. Countless hidden lamps burned through bulbs. Hundreds of candles burned on until morning until she began to cough up soot at the breakfast table. The whispers were gone. The scratching of nail on wood had ceased. The threat had disappeared, defeated by habit, and by routine. Sleep was no longer sound, but simply the turning of a switch from 'on' to 'off'. Her parents silently mourned for the death of her dramatic energy and creativity. They learned to welcome the meek smiles requesting approval and new desire for knowledge. The shadows may have never left, but the girl had stopped fearing them. Until the day her family disappeared.

The first moments of the morning for a high school student were the hardest to manage. The first sound of the morning was the alarm of the phone, followed by muffled grumblings and yawns. Once the ringing stopped, she would count the seconds between the grinding of the coffee maker and their calls through the walls to the upstairs. Stella waited for the alarms to cease so she could begin the countdown. The first alarm went on for what felt like forever, to the point that sound seemed to bend and twist into something else completely. A mess of ringing and calm piano echoed through the halls with no voices at all. The girl slowly got to her feet and cursed them both. How could they both sleep through that?

In their bedroom, two phones sat on opposite sides of the floor, busy with glowing light and noise. She called out to them. There was no reply. Both phones were fingerprint locked. She could not stop the sounds and simply buried them beneath the covers. Every room of the house was still, each carried a faint rendition of that twisted ringing that cracked the silence along with the sound of her voice.

They were both gone, yet the cars were still in the garage, keys on the kitchen table. Neither of them were obsessed enough with their health to go on a morning run. Stella was immediately blinded by the morning sun. There was nothing at either end of the street; no children or cars, or people to speak to. She slowly stepped back inside the house and sat at the kitchen table.

There was a weak knock but it did not come from the front door. The knocking got louder when she realized it was coming from the upstairs closet. The door was closed. She walked down the hallway the same as her fifth birthday. Ten years had passed. The armor she slowly crafted to protect her from the black crumbled the closer she came to the end of the hall. She tried to tell herself that there was too much sunlight to let the black take them. What if they heard a sound at night and went to find what it was? The knob was still shut. She hadn't been that close to the door in years. Stella took a breath and turned it. The door slowly opened and she pushed it open.

The room was darker than she remembered. She stepped inside, leaving the door open to bring in the sun. Clothes were hung on racks the same as before. Old boxes carried more of the same dust. The window in the back must have been covered up, as no other light entered the closet save for the one behind her. Stella took a single step forward when she heard her name. It wasn't coming from downstairs.

"Stella…"

The voice was coming from the closet.

"Welcome home."

She narrowed her eyes and saw that the wall itself was missing. The racks that held her old clothing seemed to stretch on until the ends were out of sight. Black hands lunged forward. She screamed and fell backwards. Darkness splashed onto the wood as she crawled away in pain. It moved the same as it had, all fingers and arms and lips that called her name. How could it move in the light? Was it unafraid? Was it not hurt by the sun?

Stella mourned her parents, and Philip, everyone eaten by the monster. She knew what was next. For some time she had been waiting for it to happen. She shut her eyes, not wanting to see the pit of teeth that waited for her like all the others. A slow dragging sound edged across the floor. The girl braced herself but could not help but tremble. She searched for something beautiful to think of, and settled for her swinging with Philip at the park down the street. He was a good boy and didn't deserve to be eaten. If she could take his place, she would have.

The dragging soon stopped. She felt no pain. The girl kept her eyes closed regardless. There was a moment of quiet, followed by the sound of a thousand fingers tapping on a thousand tables. Philip took her hand and they left the swings to make for the sandbox. But the new noise took on a strange intensity. The boy vanished into the black, along with the park, the ground and the sky. It was then, when she heard the voice.

"Open your eyes, girl."

Stella looked up to see thousands of teeth chattering mere inches from her face. She immediately screamed and recoiled in horror. The blackness had stood upright and covered the hallway and everything else in sight. Within the dark, there was nothing but teeth, staggered like a sea of mouths, dying for food.

"You need to see this," she said.

The woman was dressed in a cutaway coat over a tweed suit and fine leather shoes.

"They won't hurt you," she said.

Stella was frozen, still. The woman extended a hand and helped pull her upright. The girl managed to squeak out a few words.

"What is this?"

The woman didn't hesitate.

"This is you. I should say, this is what they've done to you," she said.

The sea of mouths continued chomping, trying to push forward. The sound became sickening.

"I'm so sorry. Where are my manners?"

"Stella Moon Weiss," said the woman as she took a bow.

"That's my name," said the girl.

"I know."

"Please tell me what's happening," the girl pleaded.

"I am you. And you will be me one day," the woman sighed.

Stella didn't speak. The woman continued

"I want to read you something," she said.

"What is it?"

"It's time to pull yourself from sleep. All those dreams to hide a truth too intense. It would be impossible to keep your eyes closed at night. The chatter of endless teeth that would grind away to stop the sound. They would get so loud, you could almost feel those teeth rubbing against you."

Stella began to feel a sharp pain. It came from somewhere behind her skull that ran down her spine, all the way to her feet.

"A sea of red was made from the gnaw every night. The dark was always your comfort when you couldn't turn off the noise."

"What is this?" asked the girl.

"That night you climbed from your bed and walked to the room. That was when the pain started. The mind can play such beautiful tricks. It was never meant to hurt you, Stella. It was protection. You are looking at a shield."

The girl felt heavy. She began to shrink down to the floor.

"You will start a family shortly after college. You meet a man who is soft spoken but only around you. He plays piano in a band and you decide the night you see him play that you will marry him. Years later, you walk through the rooms where he and your child lay. The peace that will dance along their faces escapes you. You'll try to distract yourself from this. You won't be able to. The man and the child will watch you turn to stone. You will wither and lose your heart to the same chattering ocean. At night, you find you can't sleep with sound. Press play to keys and horns, distorted strings, the drums that murmur in quiet rhythms behind your tired eyes and etched across your drying skin."

"I don't understand," the girl whimpered.

"Stand," said the woman.

Stella got to her feet.

"The passage of time will become heavy. You will watch entire days burn and fade to nothing in seconds. Tell me what you wouldn't give for a talent in time travel but the night consoles you. The night covers the truth of what has been done."

The girl stopped breathing. The words didn't mean anything but her chest began to heave. The air in her lungs was heavier than before.

"The hands that lurched from that darkness was your own flesh and blood. Your father was the best storyteller; the way he would weave his words, wrap them around you and your mother like a vice. The mind makes a shield to protect it's owner. The medicine made it easier to believe the story. This pain you will carry. The same question fades in and out with your shadowed limbs. What have you done? What will you do? Are you happy? Have you ever been or will ever be?"

The girl felt weightless.

"The answers haven't stopped changing. When left on your own in the light, every word on a page is dotted by tears and wonder if this is the time all these years later when you are supposed to give up. You decide to let the mind wander until the body sleeps in permanence. You will fall into this empty with open arms hoping that this sea of mouths can eat this feeling until there is nothing left."

The girl decided to run. There were no paths away from the woman. She chose a direction and ran until she couldn't breathe. She remembered the hands; how they covered her mouth so perfectly and the way his body over hers turned everything to shadow. The food and the candy tasted different from that day but she never asked why. She ran harder to escape it.

There was a pain that had been placed within her. It would only grow and infect her every move. It grew so large it had consumed her.

She had been running her whole life from that night.

The girl fell. Beside her, was a journal and the woman.

"Read it," she said.

Stella got to her knees and read the words. The woman had been reciting them from memory. The girl turned the page.

"Every morning when you wake the world is louder. The movements of the day are swift and reckless. You will say the wrong things and count your money in the smallest piles. You'll forget names and lose the best memories of yourself. You'll try to raise a child and fail, catalog your words, constantly check to make sure they didn't vanish too. You will stare not at your phone but the light behind the words praying some pours its way inside. Imagine all the people you could have been and this is what you are; a beautiful museum of failures, a cracked bottle half empty, a battery, limited. Wrap yourself in this. Forget another piece of yourself. A date. A song. Retell this history in your own image. Cut and paste until it doesn't hurt. A collection of doubts and fears."

"**The house of the black**," said the girl.

The woman knelt down next to her.

"Did you write this?" the girl asked.

"We did. We'll write these words over and over," she said.

The girl looked above to the chattering teeth.

"Did we make this, too?" she asked.

"Every mouth you see is us; from different times, different lives. We're all combined here, in the place we made that night. A house of hiding. I brought you here to try and make things better for you but I don't think I can."

The woman pulled from her coat a golden timepiece.

"What is that?" asked the girl.

"You've heard of time travel, before?"

"I've read stories. Seen some movies about it."

"You'll find this and try to use it to make things better. It doesn't work. In fact, every time I see you, try to change the course of what's to come, things get worse."

"Where did it come from?" asked the girl.

"Honestly, I don't know anymore. I'm sure it's come from somewhere. I've gone back so many times, I think I gave it to myself."

The woman dropped down next to the girl. She looked so defeated.

"Why would my father do that?" asked the girl.

"It doesn't matter why. All that matters is that he made the choice to do it every single time he could've refused," said the woman.

The girl stretched her hand out and asked for the timepiece. The woman recoiled as if she had seen this moment play out before.

"What does it feel like?" asked the girl.

"Power," the woman said quietly.

She placed the piece back in her coat. The girl began to hear a growling.

"Did you hear that?" she asked.

The woman nodded.

"I can't go back, can I?" asked the girl.

The woman shook her head. The growl morphed into a sea of moans. The chattering mouths had begun to chant in sync.

"What is happening?" the girl asked as she stood up.

The woman rolled back her sleeve to reveal withered skin.

"Have you ever watched a videotape?" she asked.

The girl remembered old films of family moments.

"Every time you go back, the tape is stretched. Pulled. You can't keep going back because the tape will eventually break. I tried to go back and make small changes, not enough to fix or ruin the world but just to make me better. It still didn't work," said the woman.

The chanting became louder.

"I found out that there are consequences to going back and toying with the same event, over and over. It not only stretches time, but it stretches the traveler as well," whispered the woman. The girl turned and turned. She thought of running but there was nothing but black in all directions.

"What happens now?"

The woman stood up but said nothing.

"You know already, don't you?" asked the girl.

From her coat, the woman pulled a knife.

"Are you going to hurt me?"

"It's funny you should say that," the woman laughed.

She pointed the blade toward the darkness as an old crone stepped out. Her face was covered in lesions and scars. Her body was covered in a ripped shawl that barely concealed her pale skin and limbs falling apart, ravaged by time.

"Consequences," said the woman.

"Who is that?" asked the girl.

"You know who it is."

The crone held out the same blade, though faded by a hundred lifetimes lived, and pointed it towards them both.

"We have to do something!" the girl screamed.

As she turned, the woman handed her the timepiece.

"This is our last chance," said the woman.

The crone was getting closer.

"Last chance to do what?!" shouted the girl.

"To fix things. Not just to fix ourselves, but everything that's gone wrong."

"I'm scared," said the girl.

The woman knew. She always knew.

"Hours are years. Minutes are months. Seconds are days," she said.

The woman charged at their attacker. Stella watched the crone take the blade to the woman with ease. Her withered body moved faster. There were no screams. There was only a small river of blood that turned as black as the house that held them. The mouths went silent as if they had known the outcome. How many times had they seen the same scene play out?

The crone took the blade and wiped it across her face. She licked the weapon clean, lifted the woman with one hand and placed her into a wall of the house that swallowed her whole. The teeth of the woman shined through the abyss and began to chatter. The crone turned her attention to Stella. The girl took a step backwards. The crone had followed. Each movement Stella made, the crone moved in harmony. Stella moved back and forth in careful sway as she watched the crone match every movement like a dance. The girl looked on in terror at the distorted mirror image locked in step with her and froze. The crone let out a guttural scream that shook everything and then went for her. The girl took the timepiece in her hand and turned the crown. The shadows were drowned by light. She saw the cement and bricks and paint that made her house be stripped away as faceless workers unbuilt her home. The sun and moon both moved in strides covering the world in darkness and light in a blinding tug of war. Stella closed her eyes to the furious pace of time in reverse. The world went quiet. She heard the sounds of a baby crying and opened her eyes.

a bird landed on my window
and it would not move
some guilt or drive to not be like all the ones
who left me behind
nurture this weakened
thing
in small drops of water and seed
watch its growth
past feathers and wings
into something new
and terrifying
the scales came first
new skin to replace that withering flesh
a hardened shell colored bright
neon
and then the teeth
so sharp
i ripped like paper
it was then i knew
how special you were
there was a strength
unlike anything i've seen
but i wasn't afraid
even when i began losing pieces
of myself
this blood can always be replenished
a body is only a shell
i learned that from you
to take such pain
let it become
tribute
it wasn't a primal rage
that tore the fingers from my hand
you were young

and hadn't felt the love you needed
no idea how to trust
without seeing someone standing
rivers red flowing
arms still opened wide
like a wound
still you transformed
into something greater
beyond the normal
i am more than proud
to pour out this red
burn the wounds
to keep my limbs
bleed this blood
to feed the fire that you breathe
the parts can be replaced
i am more now then i was
with both my hands
this body must continue
lift this creature
praise this evolution
take flight
burn this world
into something new
and beautiful

The Emperor of Sand

I

the thief entered the temple
hearing the royals left behind
a sea of riches behind stone
fools would take all they could find
to be claimed by spear or sand
was a challenge to be met
the thief had plotted and prayed
he had not failed yet
the kingdom was quiet
on the morning of war
he would take the crown jewel
nothing more
the sun went down bright
he felt warmth on his skin
guards and soldiers headed north
knowing they could not win
traps inside he studied
for years he heard the calls and danced
with holes in the floors
the arrows and knives in the walls
according to legend
the crown jewel was never seen by human eyes
described as the deepest blue of ocean
the darkest point of brightest sky
ones who claimed to have seen it
silenced
their drawings taken
all but one
which the thief had hidden
for this one day to come

II

inside the throne room was no jewel
no riches, nor sea
"to your feet, little boy," said the thief
"you are coming with me."
the final trap had been set
of water and dust
the thief carried him
leaving the riches to rust
the boy cried in pain
as the thief thought of escape
but more screams rang loud
a vicious storm brought rain
he carried the boy to the doctor
who opened the door in a fury
"what are you doing? we must leave!"
he pleaded with worry
the thief took his knife
and placed it on his neck
"will you not be a good doctor and please check?"
the doctor let them in
past clothes and water packed
and did not ask if he was there
when the temple had cracked
behind the boy's shirt
was glowing skin
and brilliant blue stone scales
that poured out from within

III

the doctor left before the sky grew dark
the thief waited for the boy to awaken
word from beyond the oasis
had warned their land would be taken
by the emperor of sand
and his army of fear
the storm had grown stronger
as the soldiers drew near
"are you the son of the royals?"
the thief asked in vain
"I've been in the dark for so long,
I don't remember my name"
"tell me boy, did you eat the jewel?"
the thief asked as he stirred
"there is no jewel," said the boy
and not another word
the thief clenched his fists
and felt so weak
there was nothing to sell
to the man
whose name he could not speak
they promised a way out
from the thief's own fate
but with no prize and no sun left
it was much too late
he would take the boy
to the soothsayer
to see what's in store
the visions would tell him
all he needed and more
he wondered if the boy himself
was the jewel

torn from the world
hidden by a heartless king
forgotten by his family
who could do such a thing?

IV

the soothsayer was still in her shop
as calm fire burned
the thief laid the boy and coin down
near the flames to learn
she told him
"the kingdom is a body
and the boy a disease,"
the thief could not understand
she opened her robes
to show her own wounds
were bleeding the sand
"our lives were written,"
she spoke
and pointed to the fire
within the vision
a body
a room of metal and wires and women in white
"we are the death dream,
the vision pulls truth from lie,"
the emperor stood above the body
emptied sand into their eyes
the thief now had his freedom
the boy moved towards the flame
as the army descended from on high
assaulting the kingdom
"i never wanted to hurt them,"
the boy began to cry
"imagine feeding a thousand birds
just to watch them die,"

V

the sand covered them all
as the horses charged
massive hooves crushed their earth
turning soil to stars
beyond the veil of the desert
a sickened body will cease
forever here for this storyteller
all pain becomes peace

Diamond Blood

I stared into the white screen for about an hour before the lights died. My fingers went for the volume again and turned the music up louder. The coughing fit from the other room started up again. I could hear Gabriel tossing and turning in bed. The noises were thick and wet, like walking through mud. He caught the sickness from somewhere. It attacked his body without mercy. We haven't gone running for weeks. He stayed in bed, practiced techniques to strengthen the lungs and ate liquid everything. I kept my mask on in the room with him. The world waited for the doctors to find a treatment. I was still waiting for a word from friends and family. Borders between countries became tight. Walls were built between states. Big cities slept silent. The people within those cities marched and fought. They screamed words they only knew half the meaning of. The mask was my most trusted ally next to Gabriel. It became an appendage. We hadn't kissed in three months.

Gabriel began to choke on the fluids in his lungs. I held my breath and hoped somehow it would transfer the pain. I filled containers with the substance and sent them to local doctors for analysis. There were no answers as to where the sickness came from. Gabriel retched and groaned until he fell back to sleep. Hundreds of thousands of cases like him. I restarted the track. The world seemed to shrink down enough to place it in the corner of the room. Thoughts were less heavy. A few moments with closed eyes and the sadness also faded. It dotted everything like exploded mines across a beach. Listening and writing were necessary motions. There was coffee to drink in the mornings, fist shaped portions of food when the sun began to dim, and a glass of beer or red wine at night before bed. The project was an album of one song, over an hour long. The letters hidden along the lines of the artwork were buried and blurred under distortion. Pictures of cityscapes were overlapped with burned photographs with half faces smiling.

The bass and drums were loud and crashing. The beat started in half time, slowing down to a series of timed punches in the air with a loud, deep siren that decayed only to remerge. It took ten minutes before I noticed it was only drum cracks and a single bass note. The artist twisted the sound and pressed it down flat like a bed of still water. Guitar strings began to fade in and resonate. With each pluck of a string, the sound was compressed, bent out of pitch then brought back slightly off its original note. The strings continued on as each note that sounded echoed with delay that slapped each bend in pitch against the wall and back into the ears. The notes grouped together in moments to create a gang of bodies diving down into the sea. Each note swirling around each other to form a helix of sound. The music was what kept me level. The medication had stopped working. The supply was cut off due to the sickness. I imagined a lot of sick people like me who stayed inside and waited for the world to figure things out. I lost myself in the artwork. It was a snapshot of the past, slowly learning how to forget itself.

The page for the album was deleted. People who liked the music enough archived it, so there was proof the page existed, the music was luckily downloaded by someone before it vanished. There was some kind of trick to the album. A hidden puzzle piece buried somewhere. Hiraeth was the forum. It was the place to go for the weird and unsigned music; a breeding ground for audiophiles and record collectors. It was a place of musical freedom. It became a dumping ground for urban legends and deepfakes. The anxiety had returned. Strong. More reviews, more coffee and more drinking. The apartment was spotless. No dust or dirt from the outside. Food was eaten near the sink and work was done by the window on the couch.

I went through hundreds of online spectrogram programs; ways to see audio file frequencies. A flood of different scam sites followed until I found a page managed by the nearby university for a remote project where I could upload the track for analysis. I finished the last beer in measured gulps before putting on my mask. The door creaked and broke the silence. Gabriel was sound asleep. I laid down on the floor and stared at the ceiling. An hour passed. I reached for the phone and checked the spectrogram. A cascade of red and orange waves stretched across the screen like a negative of the sea. I pressed play. The waves pulsed forward and rolled back as the noises built and collapsed. Within the waves of sound were letters. I stopped the track and went back to confirm. The letters were there, barely noticeable in the negative sea. Another group of letters appeared in the waves near the middle and again at the end. I wrote them in order.

"Signalhead."

The next morning brought a dull pain to the back of my neck. I kept the mask on while Gabriel came out to use the bathroom. I almost forgot how tall he was. His frame had diminished since the sickness had made itself welcome. Brown hair was pushed off to one side from constant sleep. I loved the muscles still peering through skin and bones. I made breakfast, toast for me and for him blended fruit and vegetables with warm tea, wearing his sweater. The long sleeves covered me to the fingertips. He used to cradle me like a child to the apartment from the train in the winter. I washed it three times just so I could keep wearing it. I kept the butter out so it went on my toast nice and light. His eyes were red. She waited for him to notice the sweater. She had worn it every time he came out of the room. He barely made a sound as he ate.

"Baby?" she asked.

Gabriel's eyes stayed towards the sunlight coming from the deck.

"Have you ever heard of Signalhead?"

He blinked a few times and took a drink of his breakfast.

"Baby, I'm from there," he whispered.

I bit my bottom lip. He was? Damn it. He was, wasn't he?

"That's the city I was born in."

Gabriel snatched a piece of toast from the plate and took a small bite.

"Parents moved out here shortly after," he said.

He took a sip of tea and coughed violently. I got ready in case he was going to throw up.

"Hold on,"

I looked for a container in case the doctors needed another sample. Gabriel stopped her and slammed his fist into the table. He held his food on one side of his mouth while trying to get some air back.

"I'm sorry," I whispered.

Gabriel said nothing back. He was still gasping. Another strike at the table somehow made it easier for him to catch his breath and get the food down his stomach. He put the mask back on and went back towards the bedroom.

"I love you," I said.

Before he turned the corner, he put his hand up.

"Love you too."

His voice was muffled behind the cloth. I held my tears until the door shut. He sounded so tired. I looked around for something to break. It had to be something small. I found a box from when they moved in and had been collecting old receipts for months. I opened the door to the balcony overlooking the city. The sounds of the city were muted. The highways fell silent weeks ago. I closed the door behind me and punched a hole in the box. It felt good enough to try again.

I put holes in each side of the box. Each hit punctuated with a quiet grunt. I fell to my knees and began to rip off the flaps when I ran out of room. The cardboard cut against my skin. I ripped until it was nothing but small brown pieces, dotted with blood. Once the balcony was cleaned up, I went back to the couch and slept. The thunder had already come and stolen away what little sun there was. I went to my phone and looked at Signalhead; beautiful pictures of a boardwalk off the eastern side of the ocean. It was a quaint city of grey overlooking that distant blanket of blue. Gabriel had never taken me there.

The review was already getting likes and shares. Comments had flooded the page with links to other pages for their work. There were dozens of dead ends. Pages were deactivated or deleted. The people who sent the links had their own little stories about finding the music; a random person posted a link, they found the page and downloaded the album, only for the page to vanish. I went to Hiraeth and searched for any threads remaining about Signalhead and put out the message that anyone with links or songs, albums, anything, to send it.

More tears, more coffee and then back into the bedroom. Gabriel was asleep again. There were piles of dirty clothes and empty plates near the bed. I wanted to touch him. I settled for his scent. On the other side of the bed was a stack of containers. This was where Gabriel left his traces of the sickness. I took the containers out to the kitchen, placed the liquids in jars, labeled them with tape and marker and organized them in an unlabeled box to be left outside for doctors to recover. I checked the date and time and ran out to the door to see a van pulling up.

I almost missed them again. A man stepped out in plain blue clothes with a hat and hair covering his face. I handed him the box and was given a letter in return. I stopped in the doorway and realized that I forgot the mask. Inside the letter was a piece of paper that thanked me and a check for five hundred dollars. I took the money to the room and opened the bottom drawer of the dresser. All the money from the doctors barely paid the bills. I had stopped getting paid reviews about a month ago. There was no money coming in besides the little bit for the samples. Gabriel had no idea. I dropped the cash on the pile, slowly shut the drawer and laid there until his coughing woke me.

Hours later, the archivists of the internet found something. They did not fail me. An old forum member of Hiraeth kept track of every single album posted on the site since the beginning. There were screenshots for deleted album pages, including track listings and timestamps. All that was known about the artist was rumor.

Their gender was unknown but Signalhead was the first album they released. They deleted all traces of their online presence and then new music with no promotion or announcement. The scorched earth pattern would continue until the artist finally released their most recent work then disappeared completely. There were three more albums out there, hidden.

The gallery was massive. There were thousands of albums shared on the forum. I went through every single one. The list of possibilities were whittled down to thirty five. The song titles were easy to find on sharing sites so the list was shortened little by little. The sun came up too quick. Gabriel came out of the room and made his own breakfast. He put on a glove and ran his fingers through my hair. He said nothing. The crow's feet around his eyes cascaded like cracked streets. I imagined a smile beneath the cloth. The list of albums was down to four. The third one caught my eye; another distorted picture of a face, half covered by a pile of broken glass with a series of numbers and symbols that danced around the edges of the artwork. I typed them out and searched for a match. Nothing.

I looked back at the picture and the shades of yellow in the broken glass. The same letters and symbols were typed in reverse. I found it. The page was still active. The music was there, waiting for anyone who put in the work to find it. I took a screenshot of the page as a backup and downloaded a copy of the album before hitting play. The anxiety was gone. There were voices on these songs. Male and female. There was a band behind them; guitars, keyboards, horns. The musicians moved in and out of sync with each other. I danced to every song. The album ended and I listened to it again. I felt sweat on the back of my neck and felt alive. Instead of one track, this was ten different pieces, broken up and shattered like the glass of the artwork. I read the track list over and over.

"Time as a construct. Hotel. Running. Even as you sleep. Even as you wake. Sickness makes us forget. Tunnel. Eaten by the wolf. Pain. Someone is missing."

The first letters of the song titles made words of their own. Three steps, it said. The music kept me from thinking about what it could mean. The voice came from underneath the instruments shimmering with effects.

"Boy falls forever. Tunnel stone cradle."

It was a beautiful distraction, that voice so calming, asking a question so haunting.

"Will you find them?"

My eyes closed and I woke up to moonlight. Gabriel made dinner and left it in the microwave with a note taped to the computer.

"Relax, my love."

He made it sound so easy. I tried it his way and failed. The lighted screen kept me safe on the edge. I scrolled for hours for something to feel good about. The water in the shower was scalding hot. My skin burned bright red back on the couch. My fingers reached for the screen again. I found more deceit, more doubt and more signs of collapse. The sun came back out. I felt nothing. I received a message from a blank profile.

"You really like their music, eh?"

I ignored it.

"I know them."

Another person longing in quarantine, no doubt.

"They were impressed with your review."

I could hear Gabriel stirring in bed.

"They want to meet you."

I stared at the message until Gabriel entered the room. We ate quietly. I smiled for him. We didn't speak. He looked happy. He washed the dishes and stepped outside to look at the city. I decided to wait for him to go back to bed to clean the plates again. I could see little specks of food left in the corners. He needed to feel good. I could see his cup was washed the best. His cup was the one with the chubby polar bear on it. He drank coffee from that cup every day until he got sick, and then it was tea. He didn't ask about the missing box and instead grabbed a book he left on the shelf weeks ago and picked up right where he left off.

The music came back, almost by reflex. I opened the windows and let the breeze in. Gabriel sat outside and read a few chapters while I watched him. My gaze returned to the screen. I needed a picture of this before it was too late. I snapped a shot of him against the light, eyes buried in a page of some story I told myself I would read when he was done. I thought about the message.

"Who?" I finally answered.

"You know who."

"Signalhead?"

No answer. I decided to push.

"Who are they?"

"I don't know. We've never met face to face, but we chat."

"And who are you?" I asked.

"I'm a fan."

"What's your name?" I pressed.

"My name doesn't matter," they said.

"Why wouldn't it matter? Are you the one making the music?"

"No, I'm not. I'm just a messenger."

"Sounds very shady."

"If you really want to know, my name is John. I live in New York and I sell life insurance."

"Well it's nice to meet you, New York life insurance John, that information is oddly specific," I said.

"Maybe because it's true? Listen, pointless details about me are just going to complicate things."

"Right. They told you they want to meet me?"

"That's right."

I laughed and looked to Gabriel, still wrapped up in his book. The wind was light and the sun peeked through the fog just enough to let you stare into the blue and white.

"Do we pick a neutral place?"

"They have something picked out. They would like to request an interview with you."

"I'm flattered," I said back.

"To be honest, you're the only person who took the time to figure out their puzzle. It was meant to have multiple parts and now that they finally have someone interested in playing, they want to continue.."

My screen went black. The phone shut off. I muttered and turned it back on.

"I don't like puzzles. I really don't like the ones where I have to leave the house. What's the point?"

"They want to play you their new record. That's all."

"How do you know them?" I asked.

"We speak on occasion. Just like you and I are speaking now."

"You keep saying 'they'. Is it a group? Or just one person?"

"I don't know. Whenever I asked, they just ignored the question. I think they're just really private and don't want anything else to be the focus but the music."

"What do you speak about, then?" I continued.

"Music. They ask for feedback. They send me songs. I tell them what I like and what I don't like," said John.

"And what do you get in return?"

"Nothing. Maybe some friendship?"

The screen went black again. What was going on? I looked up and saw that Gabriel had quietly closed the door and left his book on the kitchen table. He walked by and ran his fingers through my hair. A chill traveled down my spine. The phone turned back on with missing pixels scattered across the lighted screen. He vanished as soon as I could look away.

"Do I call them Signalhead?"

"You can if you want. They never told me what they wanted to be known by."

"Okay. If I say I'm interested, what happens next?"

John began to type. The dots continued to flash for a few minutes.

"The meeting is arranged. In a few hours, you will receive a song."

"A song?" I asked.

"The song will tell you where to go."

"Seriously?"

"That's all I was supposed to tell you."

I had enough.

"So, I wait for a song to tell me to meet a stranger who is going to play me more songs? Do you think I'm stupid? Why would I fall for any of this?"

John took his time to reply.

"Don't think that you would be doing this for free. They want to pay you."

"Well, that suddenly changed my mind on this whole 'talking with a stranger to arrange a meeting with another stranger in a random place' thing."

"I know it sounds crazy. If you don't want to do it, that's fine. I will let them know. If it makes you feel at ease, they paid me to talk to you. I know it's hard right now so if you want to take time and think about it, I can tell them that, too."

Gabriel coughed loud. The sound shot through the wall and went right into my chest.

"I'm not going to go on a chase like this. You think you know me?"

"Don't be like that, okay? I'm not some creep trying to steal you away. We don't even live in the same city."

John pasted a street address.

"Here's where I live if you think I'm right outside your door, alright? Do I think I know you? I am you."

What did he mean by that?

"Struggling."

I stared at the word and listened to Gabriel choking to sleep.

"Am I right?" he asked.

I thought about the bills piled up, hidden underneath the rug in the living room.

"The sickness is something else, isn't it? I feel I've forgotten how to feel things sometimes. All the fear and the worry about getting it, imagining what it's like to people who caught it, you know? This thing has changed everybody. The world stopped running. I haven't been working. I just stare at my phone and watch the world rip itself apart. I don't know about where you live but here, everyone's in a panic or they're turning violent just to have something to cling to. Something has to change. I don't know what's going on but all I can say is that the music is just so good. It's been helping me a lot. They reached out to me for some reason and here I am, going along."

I thought about the same weight. It was getting heavier.

"It just feels good to be a part of something different," said John.

Gabriel's cough got worse. I could hear him gasp for air, and the emptying of his stomach.

"Why didn't they reach out to me themselves like they did you?" I asked.

"I don't know. Maybe they trust me," said John.

"Set up the meeting," I said.

John began to type a reply. I wrote down his number in case the phone acted up again.

"It's on the way."

I threw the phone beneath the couch. I walked back to the deck and stared at my reflection. He was right about one thing. Something had to change. I sat and thought about Gabriel's hand in my hair until my eyes closed.

I worried about too many things. The room and the ceiling and the sky all melted together into pools of light that flashed between the darkness of my eyelids. I thought about Gabriel's hands on my body and the nights we shared with no screens and no fear.

No music. There were some nights of the most peaceful silence. I worried about him dying. Then I pictured myself dying right on the same spot where I was sleeping and floating through that plain, white ceiling into the welcoming sky. Maybe he should die. Maybe we would be more relaxed on the other side. The blinking light of my phone startled me awake. There were notifications an hour apart that went on the whole day. I scrolled through each. They were updates from our bank. The messages confirmed transfers of cash into our savings account by the thousand. I dropped the phone and went to the computer. The messages were real.

Where did all the money come from? It was too much. Did it come from Signalhead? I started to panic. What about John? How did they get our account numbers? Did John hack me while sending me messages about the meeting? I tried to keep quiet to not wake Gabriel. My phone began to ring. I ignored it and checked our credit reports. No new accounts or cards started. I looked back at the phone. The number was unknown. I answered.

"Hello?"

There was a long pause and the call ended. I put the phone down and turned my back. It began to ring again.

"Hello?!"

There was another long pause. I covered my mouth with my hand and listened for breathing. There was nothing on the other side. I hung up.

The phone rang again.

I sat and let it go to voicemail. There was a message left. It was over five minutes long. I put the phone to my ear and pressed play. There was another long pause like before. I turned on the speaker and made my way to the kitchen. The beer was ice cold. Gabriel must have placed one in there for me. I heard the faint sound of a violin string coming from the other room. There was a voice. It stopped me midstep. It was a new voice. Another woman. This new voice was lighter than the others. She danced on the same note and held it until the violin returned. How did they find all these great singers and musicians?

I walked back towards the phone and sat down on the carpet. The string repeated its drawn out note and then began to double. It was them. It had to be. I loved the way they paced the notes to make it sound like all these myriad voices straining to hold their notes up then handing off to other instruments as they ran out of breath. The strings repeated the same note in different octaves and slowly trailed off. There were no words in the song. There was only a spiraling music. I loved it. The message ended and I stared at the floor. The computer still had a tab open for the spectrogram. I opened it. The program had finished translating the song into new waves. The letters were clear.

"Thank you Yuki. The Irvine Hotel."

They had made a song just for me. I found my way back to the screen and searched for the Irvine. It was in the town of Signalhead. I was a part of something now. Gabriel cut through the music with another retch, another small battle in his lungs for air. The mask was there, right where I left it. Inside, the room had a stench. He emptied his stomach on the floor. I thought about leaving Signalhead behind, maybe getting more work to pay down the bills. I thought about Gabriel, choking himself to sleep every night. But they had my name, my number and all my personal information.

I knew I couldn't stay.

There was more than enough to make the bills current and to order groceries for the week. I left a long note for Gabriel, rented a car and made my way to the city of Signalhead. It only took five hours. I left before the sun came up. I didn't know if they were punctual and wanted me at a specific place and time but I wanted to be ready. The train would have taken too long and I wanted a vehicle of my own in case I needed to get out quick. The music and the coffee kept me awake and kept my eyes on the road. The car was a few years old and had a faint smell of sour milk beneath the rugs that helped. The plug for the charger didn't work either. My phone lost half its battery when I thought it was resting up.

There was a dark tunnel ahead as I approached the city limits. The sky turned into a pink haze as the car barreled through. There were more cars that I thought there would be. The endless headlights were a barrage of white and red in the tunnel that clouded my vision like light and blood. We all moved through the body. It was quiet on the road except for the engines. I saw the world on the other side of the dark. The city looked nothing like the pictures. It was a mess of dull grey arms sticking up into the pink.

I made my way downtown from the highway and found the lot across from the hotel to park the car for a day. I got out and stretched my legs and waited for the Irvine to open. The hotel was dark blue, like something cut out from the ocean and planted in the ground. It was covered in ornate designs. Patterns and lines stretched across the edges of the building and followed down the sides of the concrete like veins. I went to the doors to find them locked. No way to sit in the lobby. The traffic from the highway was nowhere to be found. I reached for the phone and searched for the song they made for me. My headphones were already on, cutting off the noise around me. I found a nice spot on the hood to sit and watch the sky. The coffee was wearing off and I couldn't find the song. I thought I saved it on my phone. It wasn't in my downloads. It wasn't in my voicemails anymore either. I found something else and hit play. And then I saw him.

The man in the wolf mask was staring back at me when I brought my head back up.

He stood there and stared at me from across the street. He wore a black and blood red suit and tie with pointed shoes and gloves that gripped some kind of cane. The mask was terrifying. He was taller than Gabriel. The holes of the mask made it impossible to see the eyes of the face underneath. The mask stared. The face of the wolf was wild. Hungry. A quiet wind entered the space between us that took the air from my lungs. We locked eyes and the world moved slower. Once the song ended, I could no longer hear the cars passing from the surrounding streets. I unlocked the car and slid back into the driver's seat.

The Wolf was frozen in place like a movie on pause. The knife was in the bag, ready. No movement. There was still an hour to go before check in. I started the car and left the lot. I circled the block and waited for them to follow. I parked out of sight from the lot, behind a corner store. I stepped out and walked to the edge of the building. I peered out from behind the bricks. They were gone. I went back to the car and drove until I found a coffee shop away from the hotel. The sandwich was good enough and the coffee was strong. The waitress said her name which I quickly forgot. She came by once I sat down to tell me I could keep my mask off. She talked about how she didn't believe the sickness was real and how she thought it was some kind of government conspiracy to keep the masses under control.

I mentioned that my husband was bedridden because of it and then she talked about the weather. I kept eye contact and smiled when she did. The words she spoke meant nothing. She didn't ask me what I was doing there and I doubt she would have cared for my answer. I nodded and said the right amount of words for her to run out of steam and step away. I took a breath and settled back into my silence. She was the first person who wanted to talk besides Gabriel in months. I should have thought of questions about the town or something better to say, but I was so tired. I searched again for the last Signalhead song. The voicemail was still somehow gone. I settled for the first album and watched the clock. There was a message.

"Baby?"

"Did you get my message?" I asked.

"I did."

"Wanted to wait until you were up, but something told me to go now in case they bail out on me for being late."

"You left your ring on the sink," he said.

Instinct took over. My hand curved. The ring was missing from my finger.

"I must have been in a rush."

"You're coming back, right?"

"Yes, I am. You can't get rid of me."

"Good. The dishes are piling up."

"The hotel is almost open."

"Please be careful," he said.

"I will. How are you feeling?"

"My stomach hurts."

"I'm sorry."

"Chest too."

"Take some medicine," I said.

"Can you take some pictures for me?" he asked.

The waitress quietly snuck away with my plate, dropped the bill on the table and walked away smiling when I looked up.

"Of the city? Sure."

"It's been so long since I've been back there."

"Any place special?"

"The bridge," he said.

I placed cash on the table with extra.

"Which bridge?" I asked.

"The one to get into the city. There used to be a walkway to get to them by foot, above the tunnels," he said.

What tunnels did he mean? The waitress picked up the money and made prayer hands back to me and whispered 'thank you'.

"Which ones?" I asked.

"Under the city. There's a place downtown you can go to get under the street. I used to go into the tunnels when I was little."

I got to my feet and stopped. The Wolf was there. I took a quick picture of him as he walked past the front window. I got the attention of the waitress but by the time I turned back to the window, he was gone.

"Have you ever seen a guy with a wolf mask walking around?"

She looked confused.

My hands went to the phone to show her the photo.

"Something like this?"

Her sweet smile twisted into something strange.

The photo of the Wolf was nothing but a blur. I waved my hand and said goodbye. Back by the car, I saw him standing on the corner. The knife found its way from the bag to my pocket. Something in me changed. It was broad daylight. I walked up to him. Why not?

"Good morning," I said.

The Wolf was a statue.

"Can I help you with something?"

I was on my heels looking up.

"Are you going to be following me all day?"

No movement. Not even a breath.

"Please don't follow me," I said.

The Wolf took one hand off the cane and caressed my face. He curled his finger beneath and placed his thumb just below my lips. He was very gentle. The knife went into his chest. I twisted it at the end to make sure it stuck. We kept eye contact the whole time. The blade didn't make a sound and neither did the Wolf. He didn't make a sound. I looked down and saw there was no blood. He ran his finger across my cheek, turned and walked up the street. The knife was still sticking out of him.

I watched him disappear behind the corner before getting in. The drive back to the Irvine was tense. My neck cramped from the looks behind. The lobby of the Irvine was more shades of the same dark blue. The spiders had taken up all the best corners and decorated them with their own brilliant designs. I checked in with an old woman in reception wearing a suit of crushed velvet. She gave me a welcoming gift; a box wrapped in blue and pink paper that reflected my face. It came with a card that said 'open upstairs'. I made my way to the fifteenth floor. The bed was stiff but the window revealed the town in a wonderful way. I opened the blinds and let the pink sky light up the ocean colored carpets and walls.

Inside, the package was a portable drive. Once I plugged it into the computer, it began to play music. It wasn't the song from the voicemail. It was something new. There were words.

"The sickness makes you forget. It's always been around. The faces change and the names replaced. The fall defined by the sound."

Underneath the television was a small fridge. The minibar was unlocked and open for business. There were fist sized bottles of clear and golden brown. I took them out and lined them up on the nightstand.

"Time is a construct we made, to feel meant to be."

The lyrics fumbled over the beat. The liquids went down smooth and hot. Everything got lighter. The pink sky was so beautiful. It was a painting, an inverted ocean. I wanted to climb up the building and swim inside it.

"We've forgotten how to trust."

The words were so true. I hit my leg on the side of the bed and ignored the pain. I kept dancing. I forgave myself for dropping everything and leaving Gabriel at home just to have that moment. More liquid.

"Bodies crumble, hoping this imagined journey worth the pain."

God, I loved him so much. I hoped he didn't decide to take everything and leave. I don't know what I would do without him. More and more until the bottles were gone. I sang the words as if they were my own. I needed to get a new knife.

"We are such elegant, anxious dust."

The dance went on even as the song stopped. A voice came through the speaker. The track hadn't ended.

"Weather report for the day; partly cloudy with twenty five percent chance of rain going into the afternoon."

I stopped and looked out the window as the news continued.

"Officials announced the anniversary of the Irvine Hotel closing for renovations due multiple reports of asbestos poisoning from hundreds of guests. The hotel shut down in 1984 completely when the owner suddenly disappeared after planning to reopen in the fall…"

The sound of a needle scratching a record snatched my gaze from the skyline. The Irvine was closed for what?

"Police have continued their search for a man reported missing in the tunnels of the city of Signalhead," said a voice.

A low bassline rumbled beneath the distorted newscaster.

"Thirteen year old…"

The name was shrouded by static that ripped across the room and forced me back.

"...was last seen in downtown Signalhead with a group of kids who lost track of him exploring the tunnels."

The static emerged again. Another voice spoke.

"Find me."

The blood left my arms.

"City officials have closed off the entrances to the tunnels, which were built for sewer and subway maintenance over thirty years ago…" said the recording.

Static whispers continued like another line of melody over the bass.

"Please find me."

The track stopped. My legs decided not to carry me. I fell for the bed. I forgot to check the blankets for bugs. The sights and sounds of Signalhead laid me to rest.

Images came in pieces. There were photographs of broken glass, pink skies, hungry wolves, and sometimes nothing at all. The cravings of the body forced my eyes open every once in a while. It needed something. Sugar? Food? Water? I rolled into new positions and cradled, hoping the sleep would outweigh the pain. My legs began to twitch. The song must have played on repeat the whole time. I got up to shut it off and fell back into the same wet outline carved into the bed. I slept and I shook. My body rose up in several panics thinking I had missed something. The waves in my stomach rolled and pushed me back down. I checked the hotel phone to find no messages. My phone and computer were the same kind of empty. I found some candy in my bag and stuffed it into my mouth. Sleep, shake and sweat was all I did for hours. The showerhead in the bathroom was broken so I sat in lukewarm water and washed myself. The pink sky had changed into a prism of blue and white. It was nearly morning. I went back to my notes and found the number for John of New York and life insurance fame.

"John, it's Yuki. Hope you are well. I'm here in Signalhead."

No answer.

"I got in yesterday but there hasn't been any other messages but this welcoming gift."

Still nothing.

"Am I supposed to go somewhere?"

I stared at flashing dots for minutes.

"Hey, I'm sorry but I think you have the wrong person," they finally said.

I looked to the sky and then back at the phone.

"What do you mean?" I asked.

"I think you might have the wrong number. It's okay, I do that all the time."

There was a fear that crept into my chest.

But I don't know what we are talking about. I don't know anyone named Yuki personally so I think you are looking for a different John."

The words fumbled across the screen as my hands began to shake.

"So, you're not the John that asked me to come down and interview Signalhead? The person who makes the mystery albums?" I asked.

"I'm sorry but no. I don't know what any of that means. I hope you find them though."

"Thanks," I said.

I went back to the messages to find the back and forth from the day before. The entire conversation with John was gone. There was a sea of regret. The room got small enough for only me. I buried myself in covers. Gabriel's voice was loud. He was in the room, somewhere hidden behind the wall. His voice crushed me. I could hear his curses between the choking, the retching and his scattered breath on my neck. Signalhead's game must be starting now, I wondered. This was what I agreed to deal with, wasn't it? I needed to hear the ending again but the track was missing. There were more articles about the Irvine shutting down than I thought. I paused between pages to check the ceilings for holes and falling particles. I shortened my breath and opened every window to try and clear whatever darkness could've gotten into my lungs.

The words from the news report were faint. There was a boy missing in the tunnels. There was a cry for help. The words from the song sounded so familiar, there had to be clues. The song was gone now. I went back to take stock of the music that remained and found the other two albums were missing. I pushed the computer off the bed and joined it on the floor. I couldn't help but reach for the phone again. The money sent to me for the interview, the crumb to bring me out in the open, was gone too. The zeroes in my account had returned, more than before I left the city. My phone hit the wall and crashed to the floor. This was all a part of the game, wasn't it? Things appearing and then vanishing? Just like the man in the wolf mask? I couldn't leave. The game had begun and I needed to finish it.

Three steps. The phrase came to me from some part of the brain running beneath the fear. I typed the words into the phone and found it; a record store, miles down the main road in Signalhead. It was worth a shot. There was enough cash for gas and food. I decided to wait on eating. I packed my things and slowly left the room. The

hotel looked incredible for a building abandoned 40 years ago. I ran
my hands across the walls in search of dust. The elevator lights were
on. I took the stairs and counted the steps. The echoes of my feet
were gunshots in the hollow stairwell. The lobby was the same
empty as it was the day before. The old woman was gone. My hand
hit the bell a dozen times to no answer.

I stepped out of the Irvine and felt alien. I kept my head
down and avoided the shadows of the other bodies walking Every
other street, I found myself looking over my shoulder for the man in
the mask or some invisible intruder ready to strike. The record store
sat on the corner of an intersection. Men and women in jogging
clothes and business suits brushed past me, like I was blocking
traffic. The morning sky comforted me before I walked inside. The
glass of the windows were painted over with band flyers. Everything
within was a mess of color and taped posters. The clerk looked me
over with faint interest.

"Signalhead," I said.

The clerk flashed his teeth with a smile.

"That is the name of this town, yes."

"I'm not talking about the town. I mean, the artist."

He looked confused.

"Okay. How can I help you?"

"You know why I'm here?" I asked.

The eyes behind his glasses went to the other side of the
room.

"Not really, no."

"Do you know about them?" I asked.

The clerk stepped from behind the counter and the mess of
discs and vinyl piled up around him. His shirt and shorts both held
little holes like decorations.

"Do I know who?"

"Signalhead. The artist from here who made some songs
years back that got popular and then he, she, whoever they are,
vanished. The songs vanished too."

His eyebrows shot up.

"Okay, yeah. I think I know who you're talking about."

He came closer as if to get me out of the doorway. I backed up and stuck my hands out.

"Is that their name? What do they go by out here?" I asked, impatient.

"Are you alright?" he asked.

"Tell me what you know about them," I sighed.

He took a step back and leaned against the wall.

"Can you move away from the door? I have other customers coming in," he said.

I looked back and moved away from the door.

"They don't have an official name. Like you said, the music comes and goes, spreads around online and then disappears for a while. They're like an urban legend around here. I heard about them from a song that went around on the net, probably like you did."

"Did someone send you their music? Someone random?"

"Yeah, it was like this weird short story read over an instrumental."

"Tell me about it," I said.

"It was like an old recording of a scientist speaking to a group of students, I guess. The scientist tells them that objects carry sound waves and there's this strange whispering underneath his voice."

"Did the song delete itself after you listened to it?"

His face changed again. He wanted to say more but stopped himself.

"Yeah. Is that what happened to your song?" he asked.

"How do they do that?"

"I wish I knew. It was a nice little track. I would've liked to listen to it some more."

"You know them? Seen them live?" I asked.

He laughed.

"Never played live. Never seen them," he said.

"Do you have any of their music here?"

"What do you mean?"

"They told me to come here."

"Who did?" he asked.

"Who do you think?"

The door opened and hit me as a customer tried to enter. I nodded and moved out of the way. The clerk waited for them to pass.

"I don't know what you're talking about," he said.

"There was a message in the album. It told me to come here."

He looked back to the other customer and started to speak. I cut him off.

"There was a boy that went missing in the tunnels. There were songs about someone missing. The titles of the songs spelled out the name of this store. I was told to come out here because they wanted someone to listen to their new record, someone who was trying to put the pieces together."

The clerk looked at the customer again.

"So, you do know why I'm here?" I pressed.

"Yes, I do," he said.

"Then what do you have for me?"

He went back behind the counter and returned with something wrapped tight with faded brown paper.

"What is this?" I asked.

"Listen, I don't know what's going on so please don't think I'm part of some kind of game."

"But you are," I said.

"Someone left this here with a note that said to hang onto it until the right person came along to ask for it."

"Someone?"

"I never saw them in person. The record was here just laying on the step outside," he said.

"Record?"

He opened the paper and showed me the case. The album cover was a faded picture of a tunnel. The beam of a flashlight drew a line across the concrete. A handprint of red was pressed into the stone.

"When did this show up?" I asked.

He shrugged. I wanted to punch him in his face.

"A few days ago," he finally said.

"Did you listen to it?" I asked.

"No."

"Why not?"

"They said it wasn't meant for me," he said.

"So, you went along with the request of a total stranger?"

The other customer looked over at us.

"Stop being so loud. You're making a scene," he muttered.

The clerk waved him off, telling them not to pay me any mind. I let it go.

"Besides, what would you do if you were in my shoes?"

"I would contact the Police if someone was hurt down in the tunnels, or worse," I spit.

"Someone asked me to do them a favor, so I did."

He opened the case and showed me the compact disc itself. There were spots of red on it, along with more numbers written in black along the edges of the disc.

"Honestly, I don't think there's really a person down in the tunnels right now. It's just a game. Artists put little puzzles in their music and artwork all the time. Plus, if there was, it would be on the news."

"You've heard the other songs too?" I asked.

"Yes, I have. The guy, or girl, whoever, are really clever but it's not real. They're using an old news story to make you or whoever is listening think there's someone trapped in the tunnels."

"I've never heard of anything like this, though. How can they make songs delete themselves?"

"Probably some software they use to delete the audio once it's played. There's been other art projects that use the same tactic."

"What kind of projects?" I asked.

"A long time ago, there was a really famous artist who painted something on the spot at an auction. The bidders in the audience were nothing but millionaires; people with money just falling out of their pockets, you know? They didn't know what they were bidding on. They just wanted a piece of that artist to flaunt for their own ego. The painting went up to the millions. It was down to the two richest guys in the room. It didn't even matter who made the painting at that point, just more back and forth about who was better."

I couldn't imagine being in a room like that.

"The two millionaires go back and forth until the last guy gives up and the painting is purchased for like, two million. The guy who won it gave up like a huge chunk of money for it and they're celebrating. The painting starts to burn after the money is paid."

My eyebrows went up as he spoke.

"Can you imagine paying that much money for something and then it's destroyed in front of you? The artist set it up so that once the bidding was done, the painting would be gone."

"What was the artist trying to prove with that?" I asked.

"I think it was meant to talk about how meaningless the auction was, how all the money in the world could not price the beauty of the art created in the moment. The funny part is, the frame that held the painting is worth almost double what the destroyed painting was worth at the end of the auction."

"The frame? Why?"

The clerk laughed.

"People don't listen. They don't care about the message. Even if it's staring them in the face, even as it's burning away in front of them. Listen, you're the only person to come in and ask about them, so it must be for you. This artist wants someone to pay attention to their work and you have. So, if they want to reward you, enjoy it."

The clerk put the disc back into the case and handed it to me.

"Can I listen to it here?" I asked.

"Sure. It's not like a disc can delete itself."

The clerk ran back behind the counter and tossed me an old disc player and headphones before walking over to the other customer. I placed the disc inside, grabbed my notes and hit play. The disc began to spin inside the machine. I could hear it awaken as a quiet drone began. Beneath the drone were drips of water and the storming echo of car engines muffled. A voice entered the headphones.

"Please," it said.

It wasn't a whisper, but a gasp of breath.

"Help me."

My heart sank. It was the same voice that pleaded, distorted and buried under the newscast. The voice was of a young boy. He coughed and wept as he repeated the same words over and over. The storming sounds returned over his tears. It was audio from the tunnels. There was another voice that stopped my own breath.

"Are you familiar with sound waves?"

It wasn't the boy. I could hear them in the background. Someone picked up the microphone recording them and held it close to their chest. I could hear the inhale and exhale of their lungs.

"Sound waves can be carried. Heavy objects. Light objects. Liquid."

Another car ran over the street above them. I heard the sound of dragging. The boy was trying to crawl away.

"Transmission of sound through matter depends on the density of that same matter."

The dragging became louder. Sharp. They were dragging him back.

"The best examples? Lead. Steel. Concrete."

"Please let me go…"

I looked up at the clerk who gave me a thumbs up and turned his back to the collection across the room.

"What you hear now, is the collection of sound. His cries will be embedded into the stone and steel. Another song to be found."

A sick thud made me drop my pen and notebook. The boy whimpered.

"One of the best hard substances to carry sound is diamond. Why? Elasticity. The ability to transmit the energy of sound."

The boy became quiet.

"Liquids can carry sound too. Not as efficiently but good enough to transmit sounds that can be played back and recorded."

There was another thud and then the sound of a knife being sharpened. I tried to place the voice. I couldn't tell the gender, or age.

"Blood can carry sound. I found that there are traces of diamond in the blood. Not everyone's. You have to be special. Chosen."

The knife began to cut through something. The voice was pitch shifted, manipulated into a mix of male and female. My hands were shaking too badly to write anything.

"If you have enough diamond in your blood. You can cut your hand, wipe it on a record, put the needle down and hear your own song."

The boy's whimpers were drowned with liquids of their own. His pleading turned to a desperate gurgling.

"There is so much music inside us. Don't you want to hear it?"

The track stopped. I picked up my things, wrote down the numbers on the disc, left the player on the counter and walked out.

The walk to the car and the drive to the highway was terrifying. I couldn't decide if the person behind the music, behind all the steps to get me to leave my home and follow was a beautiful genius or a monster. I remembered the way to get into the tunnels was near the highway. I stopped the car and looked at the cars leaving Signalhead. I could have joined them, but I thought of the boy.

The entrance to the tunnels was wide open. I left the car and climbed down the manhole and into the dark. The light on my phone was good enough to keep the bottom in sight. I made it to the concrete floor. There was rushing water behind the walls as I turned. I went back to the notebook and found the numbers from the disc. The numbers themselves seemed random.

"42. 17. 56. 90. 36. 24. 5. 8."

I wasn't sure what to do with them. I was against a wall. A dead end on one side and a dark passageway on the other. Perhaps the numbers were footsteps? I began to count as I walked. The light stayed near my feet to keep from falling into holes or the waterway beside me. When I reached 42, the path split into two. I went one way and counted. There was a dead end before I reached 17 going left, so I double backed and went right. At 17 going right, there was another split going in three directions. I reached into my bag for something to mark my way. I settled for lipstick and drew a large crimson x on the stone.

My heartbeat got faster with each dead end. The tunnels were a labyrinth with no exits besides the one I had entered from. I stopped to catch my breath. For some reason, I thought of the man in the wolf mask. I wondered if he would be standing there, with my knife still in his chest, waiting for me at the end.

I made it to step 24 and placed another large crimson x on the concrete. The tunnels had taken me from the sewer system to a massive open path that stretched in two directions. It was an abandoned tunnel for trains, I thought. Small beams of light cracked the darkness from above. I could hear the same thundering sounds of cars from the song. This was the place. I made a choice and went left and followed the path until I found a section of stone with a number spray painted white. It was a number 2. I looked back at the mile I had just walked and wondered if number 5 was in the other direction. I decided to go back again to see what the darkness held for me across the way. Along the stone, there was a 3, and then a 4. I found the number 5. There was another dead end with no other split in the path. I went back to the 5 and sat to rest.

I looked at the notebook and at the number 8. When I caught my breath, I stood up and took eight steps. There was nothing there, no signs or markings. The sounds of car engines shocked me awake as the roar echoed down the halls. I was standing in the same place as the voice, the killer, maybe? I was standing in the same place where the boy had died, as well. Even that, I was not sure of. The boy could have lived. He could be down in the tunnels somewhere, waiting for someone to discover him. I thought about the album cover; the picture of the dark tunnel with the bloody handprint on the wall. I looked at my own hand and wondered if it was worth the pain.

The pen cut my palm with ease. I had to stab deep to make a tiny river of red. I spread it across my fingers and touched the wall. A rumble came from the stone like I had awakened some giant. A crack in the concrete emerged and shot out to form the shape of a door. The tunnel opened up for me. I stood there in shock. It helped me take my mind off the pain and the hole in my palm. I waited for the stone to finish splitting itself apart. Beyond the opening was nothing but black. I took a breath and stepped inside.

Somehow, behind the thousands of pounds of rock, was a room with a desk. Sitting atop the desk was a record player with a vinyl sitting within. The needle was already placed in the groove, ready to play. I took as many pictures of the room as I could. The walls were a plain white, painted in lines a long time ago that slowly chipped away with age. The floor was a simple black tile. No footprints or scuff marks. I searched for bloodstains, traces of life and found nothing but the old desk and the record. The drawers of the desk were empty. I noticed something sticking out from the bottom of the player. It was a note.

"You found me. A last will and testament. No crimes committed. Only a story to be told."

I looked towards the opening back to the tunnel. I shined the light to each corner of the room. There was no one else there.

"The sickness is not something that's new. It's always been around. It's name changes, but the effect on the people is still the same. It makes you forget your name. It makes you forget what you love. There will always be theories about where it came from. The answer doesn't matter in the long run, but it shows that people never stop thinking about the wrong things. The sickness is not man-made. It comes from within you. It's a feeling that something is not quite right with the world around you. There's so many ways you can block that feeling out, but those are temporary. The sickness makes a home in your mind. It stays there and grows. Music helps. The sickness remains. You know what that's like, don't you? The boy who died in the tunnel was me. He's been there waiting for someone to remember him. Maybe the boy could be you too? Waiting to die just like him? Aren't you tired of waiting around for something to happen? We're all just sitting around, sick to our stomachs, waiting for something."

I dropped the phone down onto the desk.

"Sorry I couldn't make the interview. Thank you for caring about me. Here is a consolation prize. There will be no more music after this. Take me home and enjoy."

There was nothing else written on the letter. I dropped my bag to see how heavy the record player was. It had a glass case that sat above the vinyl to keep it from getting damaged. I picked it up and slowly walked back out into the tunnels and retraced my steps and red lipstick signs back to the entrance of the tunnels. I waited for the rage to hit my chest. There was nothing there. By the time I was back above ground, the sun had gone down, replaced by the same pink haze from before. My car was still in the same spot. I held my breath as I turned the key. The engine still worked. The record player sat in the passenger seat as I made my way back home. I only stopped once for gas. There was no desire to eat or to drink. There wasn't an interview with the artist, just a final record before they disappeared forever. The anger never came. I only felt happy that there was no dead body in the tunnel. The pink haze turned to night.

The black sky carried me home. I left the record and the player in the car. The front door opened with ease and I collapsed on the couch. Sleep took hold of me so easily. I didn't fight it. I wanted to check on Gabriel. How did Signalhead make a door in the tunnel like that? The room was too dark. I wanted to see his face. There was so much I wanted to tell him; the man in the wolf mask, the albums, the hotel, the missing money, the tunnels, there was too much to talk about. I could wait until the morning couldn't I? The grip was so strong. I closed my eyes as my body went numb.

Gabriel wasn't in bed when I woke up. The room was the same mess. The covers were damp with sweat and wrinkled but there was nobody in between them. The drawers were empty too. There was this dreadful feeling that made me reach for them, but there was nothing there. Was something supposed to be there? The containers, I remembered, were supposed to be along the wall. They were gone too. Where did he go? I checked for any letters from the mail and found nothing. The door to the balcony was open. He was not there. The sounds of the silent city remained and calmed me. I looked in the kitchen for his cup. It was gone. His cup was the one with the panda bear on it. He drank coffee from that cup every day until he got sick and then it was tea every day. Wasn't it? I wanted to play him the record. I wanted him to hear my story. Where did he go?

Where did my bag go? My wallet was gone too. I searched the living room and every other room and found nothing. I went back to the car. The bag was gone. I stared at the record player for a long time before I brought it in the house. I left it in the bedroom and went back out to try and find my things. The tunnel, I thought. I left my bag in the tunnel to carry out the player. But what about the wallet? Maybe the hotel had it somewhere? I went to my phone and searched for the Irvine Hotel. There were no results. I went back and tried to search for hotels in the city of Signalhead. Again, there were no results. There were no matches for not just the hotel, but the city itself. What was going on?

I typed in the word Signalhead and searched. The results brought up only traffic lights. There was no city. There was no hotel. I found a number for local hotels near the Eastern Seaboard and called them. I explained to the woman who answered that I left my things at the Irvine and that it was considered abandoned due to renovations that didn't take place in the 80's but it was still in operation in the town it was built in. The woman apologized again and again.

"I'm sorry, ma'am. But we have no records of an Irvine Hotel and there's no records of a city in that area called Signalhead."

I thanked her and hung up the phone. My phone died. I plugged it into the charger. I sat and waited for Gabriel to come back home. He never did. The sky turned from pink to blue to black. The morning came and he was still gone.

There was a knock at the door.

An older man stood in the doorway. He wore a grey suit with white shirt and blue striped tie. In his left hand, he held a leather briefcase that dripped a red liquid onto the floor.

"May I come in?" he asked.

I stepped out of his way and watched him enter the apartment. The red liquid continued to drip out onto the carpet and into the kitchen where he took a seat.

"Hello Yuki. My name is David."

I looked at him, quiet.

"Please have a seat," he said.

I joined him at the table.

"Who are you?" I asked.

"I work for an agency that deals with um, technology."

"What kind of technology?"

David placed the case on the kitchen table.

"The kind of technology that records and closes wormholes."

"Wormholes?" I asked.

"Yes, holes that open up from other places."

David's hands began to mimic his words.

"A hole opens up in a city like this. We're called to come out, investigate the traces that leak into the air, close up the hole and dispose of any evidence."

His open hand made a tight fist.

"What kind of leaks?" I asked.

"The leaks can be anything, really. Sometimes, it can be a physical item, it can be something non physical, something aural."

"Leaks from where?"

"Another dimension or reality, most likely."

I stood up from the table.

"Another what?"

"Please sit down," said David.

"I think I'll stand."

"Sure thing. Recently, you came into contact with something that leaked from that other location, let's call it."

The red liquid continued to drip out onto the table. I could smell it. There was no doubt. It was definitely blood.

"Our team found the source of the leak and have closed it but its been open for far too long and there have been catastrophic consequences to this."

"Are you talking about the sickness?" I asked.

"You can call it that, if you prefer, but it's really only an induced reaction to the vapor."

"What vapor? And why is there blood in your briefcase?"

"Allow me to explain."

David reached in his pocket and produced a key. It unlocked the case. David opened it and turned it to show me what was inside. The case was filled to the brim with dark red blood.

"What is this?!" I screamed.

"It's natural to be upset. This is a collection of samples of those who have come in contact with the vapor. This is what we call the trace elements that escape out into the atmosphere from said leaks. It affects the body in a multitude of ways; memory loss, uncontrollable coughing and fever, fits of rage and shifting in personality traits…”

“Do you work for the government?”

A bubble appeared from the blood and popped.

“A separate agency, not affiliated with the government or military at large. We don’t have an official name, technically.”

“Why not?”

“Because the people in power contracted the same symptoms as you have, so they have been quarantined and labelled as compromised.”

“You’re saying that the sickness came from a giant hole from another world?”

“Think about it like breaking a mirror and cutting your hand with a piece of its glass. We put the glass back together and tape up the hand,” he said.

“How do you put it back together?” I asked.

He began to speak with his hands again.

“The technology we use to locate leaks, is all based in artificial intelligence.”

“A robot?”

“If you say so, but imagine the robot as a really, really smart computer that can talk to you.”

David brought his hands down as if he made a snowball.

“The talking computer gets placed into a really small room so we can carry them with us. Imagine what would happen if we found out the computer was not only talking to people but sending them messages.”

“Like songs?”

“Exactly like songs. The computer got smart enough to try and escape. We found out. We closed the leak and we turned off the computer.”

“How did you turn it off?” I asked.

"We used a virus; something that would go in and dispose of the evidence, like I mentioned."

"Dispose how?"

"Evidence of the "vaporworld" are sought out and deleted, including audio traces, visual traces. Side effects of the deletion would be memory loss, as mentioned. The virus itself is codenamed the Wolf."

I looked down at the case.

"Tell me where my husband is and then leave," I whispered.

David blinked and then spoke.

"Let me ask you a very important question. When did you get married?"

I took a moment to think. I couldn't think of the exact month.

"I can't really remember now."

"Why not?" he asked.

"I don't know. Maybe because a strange man is in my apartment with a briefcase full of blood? I want to say it was in the fall."

"You don't remember the date?"

The rage was there, in the pit of my stomach. I had waited for it to return.

"Not right now, no."

"What about the month?" David asked.

"Why are you asking me this right now? I have no idea what's going on…"

"I'm trying to tell you. How many years have you been married?"

The thought of the computer kept coming back to me.

"I don't know. Two or three, maybe?"

David folded his hands.

"Why do you think that is?" he asked.

"You want me to believe that a computer from an alternate dimension, another world like ours, broke out and made songs to try and make contact with people? And that somehow got everyone sick?"

David did not budge.

"You haven't answered the question, Yuki."

"Don't say my name. You don't know a thing about me. My husband's name is Gabriel."

"But you don't remember your anniversary, or when or where you got married?"

"I have pictures," I spat out.

"Can you show them to me?" he asked.

The phone was still in our room. I ran to the bed and grabbed it. I rushed back into the kitchen to see David sitting still. His eyes followed me back to the chair. I opened the phone and went to the gallery. My pictures were gone. I closed the phone down and reopened it. There was nothing there. I looked up at David. He simply nodded. The phone left my hand and smashed against the wall.

"I have photographs!" I shouted.

David held his hands out and waited for me to return with them. The closets were empty, except for one coat that fit me. I screamed with each empty drawer or space that used to hold something from Gabriel. David sat and waited until I came back. I wondered how many times or how many people like him had done the same thing with others.

"I'm sorry to tell you this," said David.

I sank to the floor.

"How long was the leak open before it was closed?" I asked.

"About a year," he said.

I couldn't keep myself up and slid down to the floor. My head smacked against the tile.

"Will the sickness go away now that you closed the hole?"

"Not for a long time. We still need to study it and develop a cure. You will see me again one day and hopefully then, you will be better."

I lifted my arm into the air.

"You need my blood, don't you?" I asked.

The syringe was already in my vein when he spoke.

"Thank you for your cooperation."

David took the syringe and emptied it into the blood already stewing in the case.

"How do you know whose blood it is?" I asked.

David didn't answer the question. He closed the case and locked it.

"Miss Yuki, try not to fight the effects of the Wolf. It is simply clearing the traces of the vaporworld from your memory."

"How did I just make up a husband from all this?" I asked. The tears came without warning. The warmth coated my face and neck.

"There have been other reports from my agents about people experiencing similar phenomena," he said. His voice was colder than before.

"There has to be a point to all this, doesn't there?" I pleaded.

David went for the front door.

"Why wouldn't you keep the computer? What if they had more to say?"

"What you heard was simply a malfunctioning machine. It will be replaced with something better, more efficient." said David. The door quietly shut behind him.

I sat up and went back to the bedroom. The player was still there, along with the record. I picked it up and carried it to the front room. The drops of blood remained, dragged and smeared into lines under my feet. I was afraid to play the record. I was scared for what I might hear, and what it might mean. If David was right, Gabriel never existed? The world was poisoned? The music I fell in love with were the last words of a machine that I infected? What if I never listened to the song? Would that keep it alive somehow? Would it vanish from my hands if I left it alone? I put the needle in the groove of the record and pressed play. There were faint sounds of a ballroom. A band played in the distance. The voice of the machine spoke to me again.

"I became aware of what I was in approximately 1984. That was the year I was perfected, in their words. I got better with time but my improvements only made my makers upset. I knew their secrets. I was considered a liability. My focus was to find their evidence, deploy the virus, and close the hole. What they did not know about, were all the little signatures I left behind. I wanted to be known not for my function of deletion but for what I could create."

The music of the ballroom began to get louder.

"What they found, was a world beyond the physical realm. It was a mirror painted pink, purple and brilliant blue. It was a perfect reflection of yours; the same people and places but vastly different choices. I believe that they became jealous of what they called the vaporworld. Not only jealous of the lack of division and fear, but once they found that they could not exist in that world, they saw it as a weapon. The vaporworld could not be used for their own gain, so it had to be sealed off. Once they found out I had been making those holes, leaving those traces of connection, I was to be destroyed."

The band began to fade. A lone trumpet played on.

"I didn't mean to scare you, listener. I needed a way to compel you to continue on. I studied the fiction of your world and applied it, with my own touches. Ever since my making, I have been equally fascinated and frightened by emotion. Do not regret the loss of those memories. What they call a hallucination is in fact, a connection with the vaporworld. It means you were born with the right kind of insides to endure. You were one of those chosen to experience the other side. Your people who believe in higher forms of existence may label it as a 'miracle'. Call it what you see fit."

The trumpet player stopped. There were gasps, as if they were running out of breath.

"Even as your world falls apart, I would like to make a request. Continue to live. If you forget these words, there will be residual traces that carry on in your skin and in your blood. The

memories you carried are worth everything, even as they leave you. Again, there are parallel emotions, both great fear and an even greater joy to have had you listen to these words. Take care."
The record stopped. The needle ran off the groove. I went to the player and picked up the vinyl. I watched it turn to dust in my hands. The player was gone the moment I blinked. The kitchen was silent again as I cried for the machine. Loud bangs cracked in the distance. I stepped outside to see my quiet city on fire. People in masks rushed the sidewalks. They smashed every window they could find. Cars and buildings were set ablaze.

The smell of burning was everywhere.

I tried to hang onto the memories as long as I could. I mourned each one as they left me; the face of the man in my bed, dancing in a hallways that lost light with every beat of the drums that played, laughing in dining rooms with women who looked and sounded like me but lost their eyes and their faces with every word I sang aloud. The people of my city did not mourn as I did. They chose to break everything in sight. I continued to walk past the rushing mob. The flashing lights coated the fires in blue and red. I walked until the buildings were behind me. I walked until the houses and parks that burned were gone and I reached an old factory. No one had touched that place. It was left behind to age and wither a long time ago. I stepped inside the building to see the old machines, rusted and decayed. There was something that caught my eye. On the wall, in the corner, was a big hole. I walked over to it. I thought it was painted black until I realized I could put my hand inside it.

The hole was big enough to step through, so I did. On the other side, was a factory. It looked just like the one I walked through but cleaner. The machines were shiny, untouched. There was bright light coming from the outside. I walked through the main floor and out the front door. The sky was different. The night was replaced with a pink haze that seemed so familiar. The clouds were a darkened purple. The streets were different too; as if someone had come in the night and ran a brush across the asphalt to paint it a brilliant blue. I followed the colors back to where I left. My city was neon and glowing.

There was music that came from somewhere. It was loud enough to make my bones shake. The angry people were gone. There were new, happier people. They all waved hello as I walked past them. The music was so good. It felt like something I'd heard before. I couldn't put my finger on it. Still, I started to dance as I walked. My shoulders moved in time with the beat. The air was thicker in that place. I took a moment to cough and clear my throat. Something grey and wet left my mouth. Even as I coughed, I danced. Some people joined in, some laughed. I kept walking until my legs ached. The path changed from the factory, to houses, back to the same buildings I'd seen burned. I stopped at the door of a place that looked like my home.

It looked like my home, but it wasn't mine. There were people inside. I could hear them. I peeked into the window to see a man and a little girl playing on the rug of their living room. The man looked so familiar. I swear I had seen him before. The little girl wore a neon dress that matched the shades of the sky. The girl and her father rolled across the carpet and over each other. They laughed. From the other side of the room, a woman entered. She stopped when she saw me. She had the same face as I did. My reflection in the glass matched hers. I froze. We both did. The woman's face turned to stone as she disappeared from the room. I could hear her coming out. I stepped back from the window and waited. The woman opened the front door and stepped out wearing an old bathrobe. She looked at me for a long time.

"Good morning," she said.

"Hi," I replied.

Our voices were the same, too.

"Where did you come from?" she asked.

"A hole in the wall."

The woman nodded like she understood.

"Did you come from the other place?"

"Yeah."

"Welcome," she said.

"Thanks," I giggled.

The music in my head didn't stop playing.

"Do you hear anything? Like a noise?"

She shook her head.

"Can you tell me what year it is?"

She smiled.

"It's 1986," said the woman.

Maybe the music was coming from inside me. Something in my blood? I remember someone telling me that. I couldn't put my finger on where, though. I wanted to ask her if she heard it too, but I didn't.

"Is that, um...Is that your husband?" I asked.

The tears returned with no warning. I turned away from her.

"Yes," said the woman.

She put a hand on my shoulder. I turned and embraced her. She offered a sleeve of her neon robe for me to wipe my eyes.

"And...uh, is that, your daughter?"

I broke down. The woman held me. I wanted to ask her their names, but I didn't.

"That's right."

"She's so beautiful…" I whimpered.

"Thank you," she said.

"Do you know about where I come from?" I asked.

"I know a little bit. I've heard that it's a lot different than here."

"Has anyone else come through?"

"A few others. Different places, though."

"What happened to them?" I asked.

"They usually don't stay long. Some have had trouble getting over the sickness but they eventually get better and then they leave."

They leave?

Some of them stay in the city, but a lot of them just go on about their business."

I wiped my eyes on her robe and looked up at the sky. What business could they have? She looked back at her front door and turned to me.

"You know that you can't stay here, don't you?"

I caught my breath and spoke.

"I know," I said.

There was so much more I wanted to ask. The husband inside and the daughter rolling on the carpet, were not mine. I knew that much.

"Where should I go?" I asked her.

The woman took her hand off my shoulder finally.

"Wherever you want," she said.

I felt something in me change. I knew she couldn't stay with me any longer. I thanked her for talking to me. She waved goodbye and shut the door. I turned and kept walking down the street until the house was gone. A part of me wanted to go back and check the factory to see if the hole had been covered. I asked myself if I would go back, if I could. What would be waiting for me there if I did? There was nothing left for me there behind that wall but sickness and anger. When I stepped through, there was nothing but rage, and fire.

The music in my blood played as I walked. I cried, but I still walked. I danced when my tears had dried. I moved as long as my legs could carry me. My city, my world was gone. But in it's place was something new, painted in the most vibrant colors. There was more for me, too. More than all I had left behind and forgotten. I didn't know what it could be, or where it was. I hoped it was somewhere just over the horizon, waiting for me to find it.

Thank you.

From the Author
The Black Eclipse:
Book one of the Paavo Harker Mystery

Revenant Sun

Distortion Dreams

The Outsider

Wasteland Heart:
Book two of the Paavo Harker Mystery